Proof!

Proof!

(O.L.B.A.C)

Library of Congress Control Number:		2020904081
ISBN:	Hardcover	978-1-7960-9072-7
	Softcover	978-1-7960-9071-0
	eBook	978-1-7960-9070-3

Print information available on the last page.

Rev. date: 02/27/2020

To order additional copies of this book, contact:
Xlibris
1-888-795-4274
www.Xlibris.com
Orders@Xlibris.com
808315

CONTENTS

PROOF!

Our LIFE BEGINS AT CONCEPTION

INTRODUCTION

WE ALL STRIVE for validation & assurance that the "matter we occupy in space" really does matter! We stand for our own unique validation of approval; a light void from questionable debates of self-doubt, casting dark shadows from disbelief upon who we are and where we came from denial about when Our life of light begins! We all deserve **PROOF**!

PROOF is our evidence our argument establishing our truth in the statement "our life began at conception!" **PROOF** is our cogency of evidence that compels acceptation by our mind; evidence enough to establish this personal thing we each must rest assured of which is our truth in our beginning. (O.L.B.A.C.)

PROOF produces belief which rests in the truth! Truth carries no burden. The weight of denying truth becomes a burden; the longer it is denied, the heavier it becomes to bear. This book "PROOF" is written upon white pages with 100% black letters, entitled "PROOF" WRITTEN IN RED LETTERS! "PROOF" reminds you of that greatest story of hope ever told; but this book called "PROOF" proves the greatest evidence OF FAITH was given to us when we first became alive at our conception!

"PROOF" is your fact of life that has been overlooked, shunned and hushed up all our lives. Proof uncovers the fact of our "life-light" that began at our conception has been hidden under a cover of doubts, fear and the unknown and lastly simply ignorance until now. (O.L.B.A.C.) is the truth, the Holy Truth, so help me God; and God did help me and gave me the inspiration to write this book called "PROOF!"

"PROOF" is knowledge combined with Godly wisdom that was upbraided not! "PROOF" has taken in consideration of knowledge that has been toyed with and tested in laboratory using rats and documented studies that may have been pushed aside in studies and research inconclusively going on for years past and even today professional educated scholars still study and still not coming to the knowledge of our truth that our life begins at conception! (O.L.B.A.C.)

We have been denied the truth, the whole truth and left with everything *"butt"* the naked truth…. (O.L.B.A.C.) "PROOF" is now a book of proof written in black and white; it's not a bible, it's your book of proof! There may be life on the moon, wonderful maybe…yet would humans think of destroying life on the moon if there happen to be a glimmer of light shining in space? Would we discover life and let it live…only if that life is friendly…huh?? We decide whether that life should exist; if we decide it goes along with our plans, it lives if not…, then we kill. If that life is helpless as we once were; then that life is subjected to be aborted!

Yes, we would put that light out; the light that glowed within the womb from the unseen cells of the neurotransmitter of dopamine! We have refused to admit that life exists and just refuse to see the light as life even when it stares back at that light from the light, we each have within us flickering through the windows of our eyes! Where is the spirit of the soul if the eyes are windows of the Soul? Don't answer that question; just don't even think of it!

Yes, we ease our minds of truth in order to commit the act that snuffs out the candle life-light of a new being at the door of the tunnel! At one point of time at our zero hour; just when you first began to matter, your little life-light began to shine before men and they could not yet see your light with their naked eyes, but with the powerful lens that peered into the sacred of the God of life….men of knowledge saw you as a good thing, and yet did not glorify God. This life light just as well be on the moon; a city that sat upon a hill. At one point in time you and I were as a space that had no matter…but suddenly as if on a crater on the moon, we were far from being life in the eyes of the world.

Within your hands and right before your very eyes' lays "PROOF" of truth that life began as we all know in the womb. We have matured so much from yesteryear's falsehood that babies were born in the garden under a cabbage patch where rabbits nibble the leaves and the misplaced infant flown to the happy parents in a blanket of pink or blue from the beak of a winged pelican.

We have not matured enough to face up to the truth that we are still in denial of where life begins because we carry the burden to spare the rights to kill or not to kill the life-light that cramps our lifestyles!

Some things do take MORE THAN a rocket scientist to discover; and this denial is one that continue to pull the wool over our eyes and hide our face from the truth when it's staring us right straight in our eyes! Like children; you hide your eyes! You know how to put 1 together with 1 equals 2. Well that's how we add #1 once we think there is a possibility of a pregnancy…than you decide if you want it and then you deny it's not alive ….yet…then that's where you hide your face from the truth by denying there there's another number to add up that equals 2…but you can't hide your eyes anymore because the light is in the truth with proof. (O.L.B.A.C.)

LET'S ALL JUST FLY A KITE! You know to stay away from the power lines and don't fly that kite in a storm! You don't see those electrons in the air's atmosphere, but you just take that as gold in the bank...huh?? That big bang theory happen to be true when you get to flirting around with 78% of the earth's atmosphere is nitrogen electron; and you may even hear of deoxyribonucleic acid or that you are charged with electrons and you're not naturally grounded!

That big bang theory just may have made a believer out of you if you really don't know about the facts of life as "PROOF" can tell you...just don't fly that kite in bad weather or near power lines! And believe me I know enough basic knowledge about the kite and the same basic knowledge of understanding the truth and proof that O.L.B.A.C.

This book titled "PROOF" goes beyond the power of suggestions; proving the element of surprise rests in the buxom of truth. You shall know the truth; but this truth shall be hidden to those who will not see through the eyes of wisdom! God makes truth so clear even a child that is prone to wonder will not err, and a fool that has no understanding of God will understand truth and believe "PROOF" that our O. L.B.A.C.

Author: Norah G. Wilson

NOTES FROM
THE AUTHOR

WO IS ALL smiles and dreamy eyed while curled up all cozy in their bed; she could hear the shower running as she rolls over alone in their king-sized bed. Mann shaved and smiled the same "smillinginsideoutsmile" as Wo. Thoughts of how much in-loved they are together; even in silence filtered between them!

"PROOF" is so excited about the inside dance going on inside of these lovebirds; there is so much happening! The last thing "PROOF" was telling you about was the egg waiting for her concept with the sperm. At this particular timing deep within the fallopian tube, there wasn't a sight of just one of the 499 million of expendable suitors; nevertheless, the best was the one sperm that was meant to be the only one to concept with this one egg was on his way!

Almost 50% of all marriages end in divorce in the U.S. "PROOF" will prove that even the ones that stay married; the percentage of them being "joined by "LOVE" is the same ratio as the sperm race, they came from, even worse. There are about 2 more men in this world than women; but out of 157.0 million females, just one that would be the only female that would be chosen by the hypothalamus gland as a man's wife for life!

NOW, YOU CAN SEE how "PROOF" PROVES THAT EVEN THE 99.9% THAT STAY MARRIED ARE NOT happy because they are not "Spiritually joined together "Inlove." "PROOF" also proves why people cheat and will continue to have a wandering eye and heart with empty feelings without that one person.

Feelings as well as the promises made to be broken as your own words trap you on recycled paper given to whoever "takes" someone "IF" they were not "JOINED" by God. The law made by the people being just as blind spiritually as mice; "PROOF" proves they can't guarantee love, feelings of lasting devotion, they are missing something in "just" a law marriage; they really are, that one in a 157. Million that only God will give to a man!

You can fool some of the people for so long until you end up being fooled. You can't fool most people and never God. My coffee is sitting here, and I think I better take a break. One more thing, "PROOF" was asked to be written; and I am just telling it like it should have been told to you by someone who knows the truth. When you hear the truth, it will set you free or you run from the truth hiding and continue to fake happy being miserable, joining the crowd. "You have the right to your opinion; you also have your right to be wrong."

Conception is our beginning in life; "PROOF" will prove that is true, but there are more than one conception to our beginning, however, it is not like you have understood.

A "Spiritual" conception being the joining of the male and female (our parents) together "Inlove." Then there is the "Physical" conception, where the genitals come together in an intimate dance. (some couples start at this level) The Chemical___ "Our" conception is when the female pronucleus and the male pronucleus come together inside the egg; O.L.B.A.C. Ask not what it is that your Mother will do for you after you're born but know what all she did before you were born.

"PROOF" is going to tell you the biased truth, which in this case has never quite been told in this fashion before; but it's the "PROOF" and the truth, so help me God to tell this truth with Medical, Scientific, Biblical and Godly "PROOF!"

PROOF, by Norah G. Wilson

CHAPTER 1

WHAT IS LIFE?

ISDOM IS THE principle thing; with all thy getting, get understanding. I got my cup of coffee sweetened with my own blend of deoxyribonucleic (honey) lightened with half and half, and I think wow…so much to say and where do I begin! Well, all things have a beginning if they matter; matter is anything that occupies space and keeping things real and true, immediately I go to the very principle in "PROOF" that O.L.B.A.C. by answering the question fully, does **_OUR_** life begin at conception?

I knew that I must break this whole big thing up in order to get the real answer to "PROOF!" The real question that must be answered is not "WHERE DID OUR LIFE BEGIN?" I stopped right there reaching for my coffee; sipped the warm mixture and smiled to myself seeing the total "PROOF" twirl in my head.

I must break down this question, as it's not only to know where our life began, but as to much more is to understand what life is!

"PROOF" WILL TELL YOU FROM THE BEGINNING THAT OUR LIFE BEGAN AT CONCEPTION; BUT LIFE DID NOT BEGIN WITH ANY CONCEPTION OF OURS! "OUR LIFE BEGAN AT CONCEPTION. LIFE was here long before anything was made! We did not create life; life created us.

"WHAT IS LIFE?" My first answer; life is anything that has energy, anything that moves on its own force. Energy is work, and what is work...anything that has energy. I must tell you that this answer was my educated answer. Now, I will tell you what the Physicists, who are scientists say. Energy is the ability to do work that ability is to move itself against a force like gravity. There are a lot of different kinds of energy in the universe, and the energy can do different things.

The list of different kinds of energy are many; Kinetic, thermal, electrical, chemical, nuclear just to name a few, however, there is energy in biology, chemistry just so you understand that your knowledge will be cajoled with your own curiosity and do your own studying. Right now, your body is using metabolic energy from your last meal as you read this.

So, moving right along; what has energy have to do with this book "PROOF?" In all your knowledge, "PROOF" gives you facts proven by Doctors, Scientists, research in biology labs, and simply the fact that life energy never dies; neither does it end! "Life energy" began conception for conception to take place. (O.L.B.A.C.) Know the truth about what life is; understanding life is "energy" without ceasing to be. Know that life-energy is a circuit of completion that is not broken.

Let me put that word in a sentence and see what it looks like. Energy starts a new conception.???? Hum mm?? Well, somehow it doesn't get the truth of "PROOF" across; let me change it to look like this... "Energy is life; we are alive because of life-energy." Somehow, I must accept that *energy is life* **when I put it in that perspective; I understand with wisdom that energy is alive, and life is *live* energy!**

I must conclude here that energy is an element of life as well as life *is* an element of energy! Let's just know that there is a way to have it both ways; it has been proven long before I pinned this book that "LIFE-ENERGY" isn't just a *metaphysical* or a *mystical* concept of *imagination* here, but it has been proven that life energy is the energy that is present in living things and absent from nonliving things! Bodily functions occur because life energy drives those processed, not because of interactions between the chemicals that compose it.

I love giving simple illustrations; remember I am a mother of 9 children of my own and I am a pro at illustrations that get my point across the dark webs of the brain's master coordinator which houses the little gland called the thalamus into the area of where it can be processed in the forebrain which is the largest most complex of the brain.

Remember we all have been a child once upon a time; I love to touch the heart of the child in a way that carries my illustrations by their sensory organs such as their eyes, ears in this case to their cortex, making the eyes twinkle with energy!

I watch them giggle and smile or just sit still and absorb every bit of knowledge into memory and then I know they have learned what I gave to them…my knowledge! Within each of us is that child that craves knowledge to understand. "PROOF" will activate the release of emotion in your inner child as I illustrate about how our body is like that of an automobile.

Still keep in mind that in all our getting of knowledge, we must understand. We are like an automobile. Imagine any type of model; this car has a body whether it is brand new or gently used, inside that beautiful body it has parts that run that body. Let's take a closer look at what these parts are and compare them with the life energy in our bodies.

The automobile has metal for the body; we have skin. Inside, under the hood most likely is the motor or engine of the automobile.

We have under our scalp a brain; which let's call it the motor of our bodies. The automobile has an area that turns it on; it may be activated with a key or even a switch or simply with a push of a button.

Our body has no key or button so to speak, but we do have a main switch. It is an atom called acetyl that activates and deactivates proteins... Yes! We can be turned off. Metabolic problems contribute to conditions such as diabetes, cancer and obesity.

The automobile and the human body both have what I will illustrate as vital parts such as the block, the crankshaft, the camshaft, the heads, the ignition, the fuel system, being the basic parts of the engine of an automobile. The human's major organs are the brain, heart, lung, liver kidneys. Now, let's say all parts in the automobile and human body are not defective; when each is breathing or running, all is well.

Let's just remove one thing in the automobile; the *"spark;"* let's not remove the generator that generates energy from the plugs, let's *just* remove the *"plugs!"* Let's remove that same "spark" device in the body of the human; we're not removing the hypothalamus gland, but just the *"spark"* (energy)! Did your eyes light up?

Here we go right back to life energy! Without energy there is no life; without life, there is no energy. Without the generator or the hypothalamus producing the "spark" of life energy, the matter will not and cannot move or live! ***Sugar phosphates base, and nitrogen and hormones controlling cellular energy in all living matter that occupies space***! Here I just proved *what* life is.

Life *is* energy that moves on its own power against the gravity against it. What is life? We know what life is; "PROOF" has proven what life is! Even though we have "PROOF" that O.L.B.A.C. we still have the same old mindset that persuades us to not believe the truth; such as *against* believing that O.L.B.A.C.

CHAPTER 2

WHAT IS AIR?

"PROOF" HAS PROVEN void of shadowing shades of lingering doubt that life is energy of its own power that defies gravity! This is truth! I take a moment to ponder this fact. Yeah; I sip my coffee while I sit in amazement.

Why do I find it necessary to tell you I'm drinking coffee? L.O.L. I'm thinking that you may be sipping on coffee or juice, or $h_2 0$ as well right now while reading this book of "PROOF." Continue reading; find out for yourself what I found as "PROOF," that is so amazing.

I stumbled upon this bit of information as I understood more about what energy was; and then that life-energy was in places that were so conveniently available for us. God just opened my wisdom and suddenly I had knowledge that I understood!

Let me illustrate it to you. First, we all are alive and hopefully well as we were born in this world of ours; but we were conceived in the womb of our mother's, as we all were bred in the atmosphere called earth!

Unbeknown to an unborn infant; the breath of life is made by each of us once born or it is given to us by artificial means. Suddenly the newborn lungs are filled with what we call breath; but that just makes it all sound so simple, we just inhale and take that breath.

Have you ever thought about why and what it is that we must breathe the invisible stuff we call air? Oh sure, I know you have thought of how much we all got breathe to live; but what about what is in this air that is so important for us to breathe it in with not just in through our mouths, but in through our nostrils?

"PROOF" Is what I will give to you and now. Let's just examine the air we breathe that we call "breath of life" and what really is understood as "life energy." The atmosphere is just like it was in the wombs of our mother; somewhat!

There at the first stages in the 5th week of life in the womb within the womb was always the same air given, but only through the umbilical cord which attached to the developing baby. With that knowledge; understand that the life energy sustained in this conception had to have "breath of life." CONCEPTION IS A NEW FORM THAT HAS LIFE-ENERGY!

Remember "PROOF" *PROVED* that life is energy; you became a *new* life energy moving against gravity on your *own* power! A conception that had its own surplus of energy within the protons and electrons; bonded to each other also divided within themselves as they divided and multiplied in an order of the deoxyribonucleic acid.

"PROOF" LIFE was not only IN THE WOMB; but as a matter of fact; *PRECISELY every cellular activity* radiates of the life energy created in a new form called CONCEPTION! Don't let anyone *persuade* you that your conception did *not* need to have air when you were a matter that occupied space within the womb of your mother!

Conception's life energy of life lives in the constant flow of nitrogen mixed with oxygen and water; just like it will soon receive from the umbilical cord. The same air it will receive in its first breathe of life when it is born. We all got to breathe the breath of life energy! It's a *small* world after all!

This earth's atmosphere is approximately 78% and 21% oxygen nitrogen. Air has small amounts of gases such as carbon dioxide, neon and of course hydrogen. Everything we need to stay alive if we get it into our main important "gland!"

I just leaped way ahead of myself; it was no mistake, so I will leave that word there as a power of suggestion to come back to surprise you with the fact that our heart is not the real ticker that keeps us alive.

We are alive; our life support is "life-energy." We are what we breathe! We can't not have life or live or stay alive without "air." The nitrogen in the earth's atmosphere is there for the not so simple reason that it bathEs our cells with "life –energy."

What is nitrogen? Nitrogen naturally occurs in the earth's atmosphere as an element that is essential for growth and reproduction in all living things. It is found in amino acids that make up proteins, in nucleic acids that comprise the hereditary material and life's blueprint for all cells, and in many other organic and inorganic compounds.

Nitrogen is in our D.N.A. Our teeth, the iron in our blood is made from the interiors of collapsing stars! Do you want proof? I will give you "PROOF." Measurements taken of the dusty leftovers from an ancient supernova located near the center of our galaxy-aka SNR Sagittarius A East – show enough "star stuff" to build our entire planet many thousand times over!

This star stuff is 78% in earth's atmosphere and 78% in our bodies. Life has ample stardust making A.I.R. for survival of the generation of all living things for billions of years; earth can rebuild itself! This is God giving life energy, His blessed assurance.

Air is 20.9% oxygen. Oxygen is a colorless, odorless reactive gas, the chemical element with the symbol O and atomic number 8 and the life supporting component of the air. Oxygen is a highly reactive nonmetal, an oxidizing agent that readily forms oxides with most elements as well as with other compounds.

Nitrogen and oxygen make up more than 98% of the air in the earth's atmosphere. For everything there is a purpose for everything under the sun and the "stardust" on the moon too! Now that we are understanding that "air" is mostly 78.9% nitrogen and 20.95% oxygen, 0.04% carbon dioxide. Air contains also a variable amount of water vapor, on the average around 1% at sea level and 0.4% over the entire atmosphere and other gases.

CHAPTER 3

A.I.R.

ET'S NOW MOVE on to proving "PROOF" of what is the meaning of A.I.R. In one short sentence. A.I.R. is the abbreviated initials we have all shorten down from three words; these three words "PROOF" will prove to you exactly what the simple 3 letter word *air stand for when abbreviated*; where *air* is found, and even what makes *air* and why it is simply called *air*.

At this point, I'm almost persuaded to look at everything with a double meaning; and of course, you know I'm right! I've got the medical, chemical and biology, biblical and spiritual wisdom's proof to back me up. Everything has a positive (right) and negative (left) side; but that does not mean that just because you understand the positive side of *air*, don't mean the negative side of (A.I.R.) is *wrong*... it is just the side that is left over *from* not being right (positive)! That is just a little bit of "*Norah* wisdom." "PROOF" will prove that there is no wrong within the positive-negative; you make things go wrong when you break that circuit.

We are so used to saying the word air and never thinking about it being what it is. We don't go around saying to each other or especially our children "Let all draw a deep eupnea of nitrogen and oxygen through our primary organ called proboscis!

Heavens No! We take air for granted just like the beating of our hearts without even thinking or even caring to understand what causes this thing to be. Sipping on my coffee; while you read "PROOF" as your senses began sending messages to your hypothalamus gland to release some $C_8H_{11}1NO_2$- into your bloodstream and you will be cajoled by $C_8H_{11}NO_2$-!

You know if you use some understanding here; $C_8H_{11}NO_2$- is the chemical word for dopamine. I have taken you all the way from what you may think has anything and little at all to do about A.I.R. less known about giving "PROOF" about what A.I.R. is.

Rome was not built in one day; do you honestly expect me to give you substantial 'PROOF" in several chapters concerning the very life energy you have taken through your lungs since before reading this book?

"PROOF" is not persuaded to rush through this process giving incomplete information. "PROOF" will not give you grounds in which to blame me for not proving and mentioning the amount of pollution in the air that you have no doubt breathed all your life!

"PROOF" has the facts that we breathe polluted air. Just so you will know to the credit of understanding; 92% of the world's population breathes air containing pollutants exceeding the limits. Don't hyperventilate on this information; we all must live with the fact that the air has pollutants.

"PROOF" proves factual the atmosphere cleans itself more efficiently than what we cleaned our rooms when we were growing up, or what you would like for your parents to have previously thought!

Hydroxyl radicals clean the air by breaking down organic substances such as climate-damaging methane.

There is a need to clean up a **particle** of dust, so that you will have no doubt that "PROOF" is proven truth; void of any such thing as a shadow of doubt.

Let's go straight to the heart of the matter; **matter** is anything that occupies space. Space is the three-dimensional medium that contains everything that we know (which is not everything there is to know) Atmosphere is not space. Atmosphere is a gaseous layer around celestial bodies where matter density is relatively high.

Atmosphere has different types of layers like Troposphere, Stratosphere, Mesosphere, and Thermosphere. Here in the atmosphere, Sound can travel through air, water or any solid substances. Space has no medium. All vacuum. Space has no air for sound waves to travel to be heard. Sound doesn't travel through vacuum.

Only light travels through vacuum. THIS IS THE ONLY DIFFERENCE BETWEEN SPACE AND ATMOSPHERE. The light we have in our atmosphere is from scattered blue light; gases and particles in the air.

Who ever said "the sky's the limit" could not possibly have been pertaining to that air we breathe to! We have gone past the earth's atmosphere; beyond the atmosphere that we call earth. We landed upon the moon; left our presence there and returned with knowledge and understanding.

"Man made one step; one giant step for mankind marking his steps in time, but here lies the "PROOF" that the pot of gold is not just over the rainbow; our pot of gold is appearing to be far away and upon the moon.

Catching a falling star and putting it in our pockets for a rainy day only fuels the fact bearing "PROOF" we each reach our stars; in the air we breathe into our nostrils, into our lungs, and into our very D.N.A. of every life energy cell that lives!

The calcium in our bones, iron in our veins, carbon in our souls, and nitrogen in our brains, 93% stardust. We all love to gaze at the stars and watch them twinkle; but we all have that same twinkle in the glint in our eyes, the spark in our heart and who would ever think that we are all stars that have names?

We have "PROOF" that **A.** stands for **Atmospheric**, **I.** stands for **Invisible** and **R.** stands for **Reserves**. After much research and applying my heart to wisdom; here is "PROOF" that our God that has made heaven and earth made everything with a purpose.

"Let there be light" …and stars shined in the heaven while they shed dust of nitrogen; in the very protons in our deoxyribonucleic acid from which our conception was made. Our breath being 78% stars; O.L.B.A.C. from the A.I.R., one twinkling concept at a time! "PROOF" takes the mystery out of what the stardust is for; it is for us to conceive, breathe and live!

How long must we wonder what we really are, where we come from and when did we begin! We are what we breathe! Not dust mites; but stardust! We are all part of the A.I.R.!

ATMOSPHERIC INVISIBLE RESERVES! This is truly what air is! Air is atmospheric invisible reserves!

CHAPTER 4

BREATHING N2 & O2 LIFE ENERGY!

OKAY, LET'S ALL continue to breathe as I gather my information here and sip my coffee. I want to make sure you understand why we breathe air to the "PROOF" that we must breathe air to live! What is so important to breathe air?

We do all kinds of things that even stress the body out when we do what we call sporting around. I know that was not a good thing for me to write but let me explain why we need to breathe air and why I don't want to play with the process of doing so.

We all have on the tip of our faces what we call a nose. No, I did not call it a beak, snout, muzzle, honker, or even a smeller; but the nose does have sensory nerve endings at the roof of the nasal allowing us to take the chemical particles in the A.I.R.

When we breathe this activates the sensation of smell! What good is our nose other than to sit here on the front of our faces as the perfect place to rest our glasses upon? We really need our own equipment for our own personal life energy support; it's a mandatory survival device in earth atmosphere.

The "PROOF" of the matter at hand is what purpose is the nose. The nose is truly the beacon of life; the nose conducts A.I.R. into our precious bodies, as in the process known as "eupnoea." Eupnoea is the bodily process of inhaling and exhaling in oxygen from inhaled air and releasing carbon dioxide by exhaling.

We call this breathing! When we breathe that starts a chain reaction that is done without thought; this is called the body's involuntary action. Without a thought; we breathe in A.I.R. as the nose begins its designated function to adjust the temperature of that A.I.R. that we claim as now our breath flowing to our lungs.

The sinuses begin to drain as the nose creates both warmth and moisture to humidify the breath, as well as clean the breath. The nose ears and throat are partners linked by the Eustachian tube. A canal that links the middle ear with the back of the nose also connects the middle ear to the nasopharynx, which consists of the upper throat and the back of the nasal cavity. The nose is truly the *beacon* of life energy to say the least!

The nose has the perfect anti snot removal system; you may wrinkle your nose at me saying this but keep it real; you know perfectly well what I mean, and you know it's true. That nose is a hanky for snot! Remember I have had 9 children and my share of runny noses wiping their snot out of their faces when they couldn't or wouldn't blow!

That nose is really part of a natural built-in mask necessary for life in this plane we call earth. We have been made aware of the moon's low antigravity pull. We must have spacesuits that go along with our necessary source of life energy and abilities to breathe it in as our only known natural environment given to us by God to breathe and live off the atmospheric invisible reserves. Our living bodies must always have A.I.R.;

"PROOF" there is no living life breathing energy on the moon, because there is no "air" to breathe but there is "A.I.R." on the moon! There is no oxygen on the moon! There is "PROOF" proves that there are too few molecules to bounce around to generate heat; "PROOF" also assures us all that there can be no heat on the moon. No striking a match to produce a fire; remember there is no air. At least none that is to be eupnoea without a spacesuit while on the moon.

If you happen to think you saw a man sitting on the moon you may not have been off your rocker. He had to have on a space suit; without that space suit, he could only last 15 seconds before he would freeze to death while holding his only A.I.R. breath! There on the moon lays the dust from stars that generates A.I.R.

The Atmospheric Invisible Reserves cannot be breathed *on* the moon; you have to wait for it to be delivered to earth's atmosphere and time for O.L.B.A.C. to breathe it.

"PROOF" was getting around to telling you about the *vile* temper of the moon! The moon is truly a beast with a temper when you understand the temperature when the sun goes down; the moon's temperature can dip to minus 243 F. That is minus 153 C. the moon is always appearing to be sleeping from hypothermia!

"PROOF" had to "PROVE to you that we were conceived not *to adapt to* this A.I.R. as aliens, but we were conceived as earthlings by conception of this A.I.R. The A.I.R. did not adapt to us; we have the inborn natural abilities being conceptions of this A.I.R.

Over the course of time we have enveloped and developed the means of survival and morphed and adapted from that very moment O.L.B.A.C. Our very beginning of our life started from the chance of time; the power of life energy to change against all odds from the force of gravity within the cells that ignited and bonded in a morph of new life when our O.L.B.A.C.!

"PROOF" validates the war we each have struggled through from numbers reaching 500 million sperms dying silently as they *alone* struggled to maintain life energy within. Long before we felt the fire of A.I.R *scorch* our lungs as the very chemical of acid that is very well known to medical and biologists to be!

We developed immunity to the hormonal acid that by nature of hostility morphed to being silent friendly fire; wave a flag of peace in the valley for just *one* warrior, neither brave nor strong, but just *chosen* by life energy! Where is our honor from emerging into this atmosphere called earth?

Our arrival was just another battle to live; forced to eupnoea, lest we die? O.L.B.A.C. and the quest for life goes on from the valley of death in the pits of our mother's womb to the vast pit we call home in which we all continue to breathe air from which comes from A.I.R. flowing freely to each of us from the dust upon the moon.

CHAPTER 5

LIVING ON BORROWED TIME

MUCH IS YET to be written here in this book called 'PROOF" concerning O.L.B.A.C. My mind has been lingering on a screen. This screen is lit up with lights that catch my senses sending an array of uncertainties to my brain. This screen is the face of a monitor.

Monitors are used in everyday uses in our normal lives; what would we do without them? My eyes have often studied the messages that constantly report from the subject at hand back to the screen.

My ears are picking up sounds that make me feel uneasy as I am aware that the sounds would be alerting of sudden changes. I held my breath as my eyes and ears gave me a sensatory respect after a few days mixed with hoping the small bits of understanding of this humming relaying that all was as well as could be expected. My cautious relaxations often were interrupted by the sudden beeping and the flashing of lights with the Nurse appearing in the room.

Most of the time they would push a button to reset a machine, or adjust a tubing, or just speaking to me about things were fine and a assuring smile noted on their face in my direction as rushing out as they often rushed in leaving me alone with humming of the machines and the bitter sweet peace within me.

I sighed a breath of cautious relief; accepting the little knowledge I had with understanding that all the humming and purring assured us all that life was still in the patient lying still accept for the rising and falling of his chest; under the stark white crisp sheet, on the bed on his back silent with closed eyes.

Hospitals are a place that cares for the ones in need of medical care. My dad was in need of medical care when he suffered a stroke. For 22 days I sat and watched the screen; and somehow the screen became less frightening as the humming was translating to me assurance that dad was still living. I did not know at that time what I know now, and my understanding is far beyond that of the frightened woman held captive to fear of life and death processes in the body.

I did know that the screen was monitoring my dad's heart rate and blood pressure and body temperature. I understood the fact that the brain waves had to be monitored. I did not understand then what *happens* to determine "brain death."

My Dad's heart was beating; the life support was doing all the work for his lungs to continue to push his chest out and giving me the signal to breathe easier, understanding of my Dad being alive!

I was later called to attend a meeting with the Physicians concerning the condition of my Dad and what we must decide to do next. There is a lot of pressure and emotion with the respect of being family and next in kin; I was petrified, not to mention of how I was feeling sick myself.

It was a cold day in November as I headed to the hospital with my 8 children! My baby was just about to turn a year old and was happy to be snuggled inside my arms being carried into the hospital even as I realized how very tired and hot, I was feeling.

I had my Dad on my mind, but I believe God speaks to my heart as he did that instance; I was being led to just get checked out in the emergency room, my chest hurt. The Dr. smiled kindly at me as I told him how I felt, but I needed to go upstairs to be with my Dad who was on life support and I also had to meet the team of Doctors.

The Doctor then looked into my eyes intensely; his smile departed. He spoke in a very straight forward manner with no doubt arising in his words he said to me "If you don't go home and get some rest, *you* will be in the hospital____you are terribly congested____I'm surprised you don't have pneumonia!" He wrote me a prescription for my condition, and I went home, but not before I spoke with the panel of Doctors concerning my Dad.

CHAPTER 6

LIFE AT THE END OF THE TUNNEL

MY STRENGTH FELT small and drained as I made my way up the halls and confronted with the Nurses' station where several heads looked my direction as I tried to brace myself for this meeting. I was greeted instantly with information of where to wait.

The conference room was big with soft blue walls, a large wood grain table with metal grey padded brown office chairs all around it. I took a seat. The room was cool, but I felt overheated inside and my hands were cold; I stuffed them in between my knees in a nervous fashion and waited.

Suddenly the door opened; my oldest brother came into the room led by a Nurse who looked at him rather inquisitively, but politely invited him to sit down. Here I must say that funerals, hospitals, weddings and family reunions are toxic gatherings for some of us. In this case; toxic was putting it mildly! We came from a family of 4, including myself. Being the youngest of the family; leaves me being no baby at the age of 40 at the time.

My Dad and Mother had 4 children during their marriage that began their separation the very instance my Mother told my Dad she was pregnant with *me*! I was the straw that broke the camel's back! I was the flood that broke the dam; for years I blamed myself as the cause for their divorce, "not!" Dad left my mother also with my 2 sisters and *this* brother that just sat down across from me at the other side of this long conference table. I felt my pulse race to match my emotion as my heart pounded inside my congested chest sounding as hooves of wild horses running into battle.

We had seen each other a couple of days ago; I picked him up from where he had served his time of 21 years in a correctional facility. We with a common ground of being the only family members that cared to be present at this meeting were also practically strangers as the opening of the door broke the silence between us where words had not yet been uttered.

I expected a group; but only one tall thin casually dressed male walked over to a chair with a space of 2 chairs away from my brother, offered his long-outstretched hand to me first then to my brother. The Doctor then introduced himself as my brother perched intimidatingly on the edge of his chair; tipping the metal chair on one back leg with perfect balance skillfully from years of isolation, now flooding this conference with his spirit of vengeance.

I was the baby daughter in my parent's marriage. My brother was the *first* son in their marriage, being the oldest but not the only son of all our father's children. We were the only (children) of his descendants that were present here today; waiting to decide.

Dad had requested the burden of this finale decisions that laid upon his heart months ago then, would be his last wishes for me to grant now! My dad had a companion, but even after 18 years together, she quickly but bluntly told the attendants that I was his next in kin; I knew that was a slick move to make me the respectable-responsible party!

The Doctor professionally explained on our level that our father was given several tests that showed that at this time it was to be decided if he could breathe on his own and reduce the oxygen that was given to him through a tube; and remove the other life support machines.

The Doctor took it all in to account when he stood up and looked directly at me and stated that our father had me as his power of attorney over his affairs and the final decision was what I thought best for carrying out our father's wishes. My brother got his wishes met out of respect that he was the only son between our parents, but not of the only children our father had with other marriages.

I felt like I would pass out from stress and being sick myself. We both went to our father's bedside where I laid my head on his chest that went up and down with his breathing support machine's efforts. For the next 24 hours I prayed that my Dad would still be breathing as the oxygen and the other life supports were finally removed.

It seemed as if I were holding my breath on the second day; I stood watching my Dad's chest barely appear to move, faintly, but yes! The Doctor took me aside to explain that there were going to be a test for brain activity; my Dad's test showed his brain was absent of activity and I was told this before I went home. I stayed with my Dad until I felt so tired and feverish knowing it was more than wishful thinking that got me home and all my children fed and into bed myself.

I was married living more like a single mom with a traveling husband; who traveled more than he lived with me. Now is an example of times that I learned that life is not how I make it, and hardly how I took it; but measured out by the grace and faith of God. Suddenly I heard my Dad's voice playing back in my mind saying in his weakened ruff-gruff voice "it's funny, the very one that I didn't want was the very one that I needed and was here for me in the end!"

I got a call at a little past 10p.m. that night from the hospital; the jolting despairing news was being told to me gently, Dad had stopped breathing, his heart had stopped beating and had died! I shared this personal story with you to touch your heart with the "PROOF" we all have witnessed something like this in bits and pieces in living and breathing this A.I.R.

I know my Dad was gone from this life; but "PROOF" is leading us to reach for the knob on the door while turning it just as "breathe escapes freely in an invisible pathway to *where* in the world life goes once it leaves the body with the last breath!

Life energy cannot die! The life we breathe is energy given in an instance of eupnoea; by faith we let it go at the end of the tunnel where there is indeed life energy. The tunnel is in the womb of time; in faith we give life energy to someone else to eupnoea where life energy circuit begins and meets without the circuit ever being broken! "PROOF" bears witness to the old gospel hymn; noting that the family has a circle; but life energy will not be broken as a circuit in disguised! "PROOF" will prove that there is life after it leaves the body; there is more to life than with a beating or stopping of the brain. *Our* life began at conception, but *life* was alive *before* our conception.

CHAPTER 7

THE CIRCUIT IS UNBROKEN!

*I*T'S NOT AN easy thing to do to decide what to believe or do when the Doctors tell you that someone you love is "brain dead." It's not believable at all when we see their chest going up and down with the power of suggestion that they are alive and breathing!

We look at the monitor and then back at the Doctor; we tell that Doctor that we don't want to "pull that plug!" No, don't take them off that life support machine; brain dead, but their heart is still beating and appearing to be still breathing with the help of the machines.

What is the power of suggestion disguising the element of surprise? The lack of knowledge & understanding; disguising when and where death accrues! In the heart; or deep set within a small gland of the brain?

What is it that we don't know to understand here? "PROOF" will remove the veil of confusion and explain to you the simple, proven truth medically, scientifically and biblical from scholars of sound mind who have tested and researched rats, pigs, man and mankind.

"PROOF" cuts through the red tape to give you the bare truth on the matter of when a person is dead or alive! What does brain dead mean when the heart is still beating, and the life-support **machine** is still **giving** oxygen?

"PROOF" once again must go beyond the propaganda of emotion and present the truth about the heart; that continues to beat, after the **brain** is dead! The heart is not **all** that matters when it comes down to what's really calling the shots that makes the heart **start and continue** to beat!

Let me ask you a simple question; what makes the heart to beat in the very beginning? To answer that question, we must respect the abilities of the heart with **our understanding that the heart's electrical system** is responsible for making and conducting signals that trigger the heart to beat; without you thinking, however this is part of your **involuntary** action of your **central nervous system**.

The heart is controlled by the two branches of the autonomic (involuntary) nervous system. The sympathetic nervous system (SNS) and the parasympathetic nervous system (PNS). The sympathetic nervous system (SNS) released the hormones (catecholamine-epinephrine and norepinephrine) to accelerate the heart rate.

Under the brain has **2 main parts**; the central nervous system is made up of the **brain** and **spinal cord**.

"PROOF" will go on to tell you that the brain gets to take a small break from telling the heart to beat because the heart will actually beat all by itself; "PROOF" that's why your coworker acts like he can't think today, doing that brain-fog!

There is something in the heart called automaticity. That means that the heart, even if it's disconnected from the brain, will continue to beat at a set rate—something called the intrinsic heart rate!

The heart has its own electrical system that causes it to beat and pump blood. Because of this, the heart can continue to beat for a short time after brain death, or after being removed from the body. The heart will keep beating as long as it has oxygen.

Think of this "PROOF" the next time you say you "laughed your head off" while saying you can't breathe and gasping for breath. How many times have you said or heard it said "I've almost laughed till I died? How many times you said "stop, let me get my breath; I couldn't breathe I was laughing so hard with tears running from my eyes? "PROOF" will tell you that too much laughing for an asthmatic person is not good!

The serious part of the "PROOF' is that a person brain dead on the **ventilato**r is only provided with enough **oxygen** to keep the heart beating for several hours. Without this **artificial** help, the heart would stop beating.

"PROOF" also proves a patient in a coma who continues to have brain activity and function; is **not** brain dead! When brain death occurs, all brain function ceases and there is no chance of recovery.

Before brain death is confirmed, everything possible to save an individual's life is done. **After diagnosis of brain death** is made there is **no** chance of recovery. When brain death has been declared; there is no feeling of pain or suffering. *The heart can continue to beat if supported with life energy A.I.R, (life support machine) but the heart will beat only for a short time if the person is "brain-dead."*

The heart has been proven by "PROOF" while keeping all things in perspective is willing to keep beating. "PROOF" proves how giving mouth to mouth respiration when a person's heart stops (artificial respiration) is so vitally important as a means of assisting or stimulating respiration, a metabolic process referring to the overall exchange of gases in the LIVING body by pulmonary ventilation, external respiration and internal respiration when the brain is still alive.

CHAPTER 8

POSITIVE-ABSOLUTE-INVOLUNTARY-LIFE

ET'S TAKE A long concentrated sip on our beverage as "PROOF" proves that O.L.B.A.C.; taking you step by step into the proven truths that have been laid before us, but we just never bothered to put it all together as will be done here in this book of 'PROOF."

Keep in mind that "matter is anything that occupies space; and that we only began to matter only at our conception. Need me to say that many of you don't accept you matter even then. I am very excited to the point of overflowing with knowledge and wisdom in this book of "PROOF!"

We all cross our hearts in truth and hope to die if we are caught in a lie. We put so much trust in the heart of emotions and even more trust in the thump-thump that goes on within the chest of each of us involuntarily. How wonderful that life goes on without as much as an effort of us thinking about it twice.

What is involuntary? Involuntary action is one which the conscious choice of an organism. It occurs specifically in response to a stimulus; it will be known as a reflex. Involuntary actions are opposite of voluntary actions that occur because of choice.

We all have our own choices that we voluntarily make, but "life energy" did not leave some things up to us to decide; involuntary actions are those that send messages throughout our body to keep us healthy happy and alive which supports new life within our cells.

We all very well know how easy it is to hold one's breath; children hold their breath when they don't get what they want, which can be a terrifying experience for a parent, while playing hide and go seek as a child, and the child hiding holds their breath trying to not be heard or seen while the seeker is huffing and puffing and breathing down their backs screaming at the tops of their lungs_____ "There you are___I found you!"

Some trained persons were able to hold one's breathes underwater called "Seals;" "PROOF" can prove this breath holding challenge ranges from childhood stubbornness, games to the skilled swimmer and servicemen("THANK YOU FOR YOUR SERVICE!") trained to save lives.

"PROOF" proves that even musical instrumentals that require holding one's breath not only requires skill but puts stress on the hypothalamus gland to eventually force the person to breathe by the involuntary action of the brain's central nervous system.

Think back on the monitor displaying the vital signs of the body working while on life support machines. "PROOF" explained how the heart can beat for a short time without the brain if it is supplied with oxygen; but life did not start beginning with the heartbeat! Life does not end with the ending heartbeat either!

Did life begin just with a beating heart? No! Absolutely not! Life did not just begin as a monitor displayed a wave of electricity of a beating heart at the 5th week from conception. Why is a person declared "brain-dead" when his heart is still beating?

Why must the heart finally die without the brain? Where is that area in the brain that the Doctors look at when they scan the brain for signs of life? What tells the Doctors a person is "brain dead?" "PROOF" answers all these questions and even more; according to the medical, biblical and wisdom of God!

CHAPTER 9

THE HEART OF WHAT MATTERS!

WHY IS THE brain scanned for life when the heart is beating? "PROOF" proves the beating of our heart is not the beginning of our lives or even that there is life in the body on life support machines! We think that the only thing that matters is our beating heart. In science class we were taught that matter is anything that occupies space, and as far as most of us think, the heart is all that occupies the body that seem to matter when detecting a pregnancy, and when someone is noted to be alive.

According to Norah Wilson, you have the right to your opinions; everybody has the right to be *wrong*.

All of us were born to learn the first name for our Mother; "Mama," then we learned that was not her name! The heart of the matter is where we all have our opinion, in our own heart; but there is more to the heart and Mama than meets the ear and eye.

Where does life begin in us to make us live? Where does life begin for each one of us? How can such a small four-letter word be so big to trace its beginning? All these questions have been asked by us all and "PROOF" answers them all in one book!

Let's get to the heart of the matter that really is matter. We all hold on to matter as we follow through space and finally floating towards the light at the end of the tunnel where there is the be all that begins all. Life greets us all in a circuit that when we breathe our last breath; we only give back what was given to us.

What is life; life is not death that's for sure! Life is electrical energy; where is life found in us? For sure life in everywhere in us, but that final spark of life is only found in the very source where it first began. Our life must have clearly begun long before we took our first breath. Understand that we can know where our life began finally knowing and believing that the womb has life where the conception began for us all. (Test tubes respected)

Let "Proof" take you by your hand, turn each page with your index finger and read with understanding every word written here proving O.L.B.A.C. The same spark that clearly thrills the brain continues to do so even unto the entrance out of this world. If you believe that God will never leave us and will never forsake us and will be with us even unto the end of this world, then here's "PROOF" that is true.

The eyes are windows to the soul; we can see the spiritual glint of life's energy there. Whether the energy be viewed as happy, evil, loving or weak or strong; life can be seen in the eyes. Follow me inside the windows of the eyes of the experts, leaving your body to be examined and become surprised at what is found.

Here we will understand that life is not merely breathing once born; but life is in the womb supplied by the mother. "PROOF" of the matter of life goes farther than even before implantation can begin; you were alive and well.

Where does life begin if not when we take our first breath at birth; or at the Week of life in the womb, or when we dare say even before the heart began to beat, we were a living matter. A matter that was alive and occupied space within the atoms of our mother ship! Our own paternal mother!

Understand the mystery as the secret unfolds that O.L.B.A.C. at the very core of matter. That spark that we know is in our heart, in our brain and pin pointed down to a computer artwork of your head showing the left side of our brain just below the thalamus and above the pituitary gland attached to a stalk is a small gland and part of the limbic system. In the terminology of neuroanatomy, it forms the ventral part of the diencephalon about the size of an almond.

This gland is an important area in the center of the brain. It plays an important role in the hormone production and helps to simulate many important processes in the body; this gland has a target organ; the pituitary gland.

I have on purpose refrained from giving you the name of this small almond size gland; just wanted to hold your attention for a while as "PROOF" gives you the facts. More vital information about this gland and I will give you the mystery name.

This small mystery gland in the brain controls ANS, CENTER OF EMOTIONAL RESPONSES, BODY TEMPERATURE REGULATION, REGULATION OF FOOD INTAKE, REGULATION OF WATER BALANCE AND THIRST, REGULATION OF SLEEP-WAKE CYCLES, CONTROL OF ENDOCRINE FUNCTIONS.

These seven areas of the body are controlled by this secret GLAND. Let me remind you of the small sized gland that of a sweet almond; and the fact that you cannot live without it! The main purpose of this gland is to keep the body healthy and blissful by the hormones that are produced and secreted by this gland carrying messages throughout the body.

Since the heart is what we are all so fascinated with from birth to the very aged; "PROOF" will just prove what is so vitally important to the health and happiness of the heart that it cannot do without this gland that I will keep under top secret, but "PROOF" will give you a hint; the name given to this gland means "to sit under."

This gland sits in the center portion of the base of the brain; just under the Thalamus gland, but between also the pituitary gland. Working constantly even before there was a beating heart; long before there was nothing more than the neuroectoderm of the forebrain in the early embryo, which is the primary brain vesicle that divides to form two secondary brain vesicles, telencephalon (end-brain, cortex) and diencephalon.

Development also occurs differently in male and female in this area of the embryos, described as part of neural sexual dimorphism. "PROOF" has gone through much effort to keep you abreast on the duties and the site of this gland; it is also aware of the knowledge that have taken years to obtain in order for "PROOF" to elaborate the facts you are reading now! There is much anisotropic growth in the development of the basal gland; such as the adult's gland is subdivided into distinct domains; pre-optic, anterior, tuberal and mammillary.

Each domain harbours an array of neurons that act together to regulate homeostasis! The embryonic origins and development of neurons remains enigmatic. Since this gland that "PROOF" will soon tell the name of is difficult to access, many questions regarding development and plasticity of this nucleus remain.

Different environmental conditions, including stress exposure, shape the development of this important nucleus has been difficult to address in animals that develop in utero. Let's sit back and take a bird's eye view at this **secret gland** and call it by name! **THE HYPOTHALAMUS** *GLAND!*

CHAPTER 10

THE "H. G."

PEERING THROUGH LENS guided by the skilled masterminds down through time long before I was born; trained eyes have delighted themselves in the studies of the "be all that ends all" that have caused many of masterminds to be baffled and confused while drinking coffee and burning the night oil.

It appears those little hidden neutrons were doing things that light up not only the universe atmosphere, but inside our bodies in every cell of our deoxyribonucleic acid. What would matter without these particles of matter that occupy space within us? Excuse my pun!

As "PROOF" lets you look through the powerful lens of these sacred microscopes and see for yourself; you will get more than a bird's eye view, more than speculation, you will have your own wonder and understanding!

"PROOF" understanding that you cannot live without this hypothalamus gland, even it is measured up to the size of a nut... it is not a nut! I would like to add my opinion here and say that with the knowledge and understanding of the hypothalamus gland and its marvelous duty.

I would not use an almond to suggest the size of the hypothalamus gland because that made me think of our brain as a "NUT! Even though we have called each other "NUTS" … I just wonder if the medical world has a joke going on, understanding that the almond is not a nut at all, but a drupe! That's even sounding worse; L.O.L. A drupe? What is a drupe? I just told you, it's an almond!

However; since I am so dramatic, I sized up an almond with my finger and I would take the first section of your baby finger equaling up to the size of your own hypothalamus gland; of course this is "Norah's input" so don't get carried away and think your hypothalamus gland is a super big almond butter finger!

After I tell you about the almond, you will believe the medical field gave the hypothalamus gland a compliment comparing it to the almond's size.

I realize I told you that "PROOF" is going to give you the truth about things concerning O.L.B.A.C. This is getting to that; just bear with me a little more. I declare this is very important or I wouldn't waste our time with this little, but important input!

The Almond is truly amazing! I am surprised the King Solomon did not compare his beloved like unto the almond of his emotion; could it be that he was already under the control of the hypothalamus gland?

As the first flower of the year the blossom is the awakener, hence it depicts watchfulness; it also represents sweetness, charm, delicacy. The Chinese sees the almond as feminine beauty, fortitude in sorrow, watchfulness. In the Christian tradition, the almond signifies divine favor and approval, and the purity of the virgin.

The almond is a drupe, consisting of an outer hull and a hard shell with the seed, which is not a true nut, inside.

The almonds are in the peach family. This category of stone fruit itself is a member of the prunus family. Stone fruit encompasses trees and shrubs that produce edible like cherries, plums, peaches and nectarines. The almond is a fruit; 3.5-6 cm (1 3/8- 2 3/8 in.) long.

Now that you have all this knowledge about the almond; compare this with the center part of the brain that is called the hypothalamus gland! I have you to know right now that "PROOF" is on point with the proof that the brain is the flower or the blossom that is the body's watchman day and night.

Of course this little almond shaped organ has its own charm and sweetness right down to the hormones released from the pituitary gland; releasing the true fortitude bold and full of favor as it religiously keeps a watchful eye over the matters at heart, mindlessly attending our vital signs involuntary actions! (Join me in another sip of coffee)

Our good old hypothalamus gland is deeply embedded in the harden shell as the almond in prunus family; consisting of an outer hull (the skull) which is a hard layer of bone, and three layers of tissue called meninges. The strong outer layer is named the dura mater. The middle layer, the arachnoid mater, is a thin membrane made of blood vessels and elastic tissue. It covers the entire brain.

The hypothalamus gland; the gland we cannot live without, maintains homeostasis, form myelin and facilitate signal transmission in the nervous system. Destruction of the regions of the brain will cause "brain death." Without the key functions, humans cannot survive.

The hypothalamus is a small structure that contains nerve connections that send messages to the pituitary gland. The hypothalamus handles information that comes from the autonomic nervous system.

It plays a role in controlling functions such as eating, sexual behavior and sleeping; and regulates body temperature, emotions, secretion of hormones and movement. The pituitary gland develops from an extension of the hypothalamus downwards and from a second component extending upward from the roof of the mouth.

As "PROOF" has proven that the hypothalamus gland gets its name from the thalamus gland, and it sits between the nearby pituitary gland; it is only fitting to give respect to them here right along with each other.

The thalamus serves a relay station for almost all information that comes and goes to the cortex. It plays a role in pain sensation, attention and alertness. It consists of four parts; the hypothalamus, the epithalamus, the ventral thalamus and the dorsal thalamus. The basal ganglia are clusters of nerve cells surrounding the thalamus. "PROOF" proves this is backed up by K.J.V. "The race wasn't given to the swift, neither was it given to the strong; but to him that endure unto the end." The hypothalamus gland endures unto the end, long live the H.G.

CHAPTER II

"HYPOTHALAMUSLY" SPEAKING!

I HAVE BEEN working diligently, often pausing to marvel at the knowledge "PROOF" has proven; yet the best is yet to come proving O.L.B.A.C. "PROOF" knows that life energy is alive and in all living things; moving on its own energy against the force of gravity. "PROOF" has given you absolute proof that **A.I.R.** is **Atmospheric Invisible Reserves**; reserves that we so casually referred ourselves as **airheads** call air!

"PROOF" has taken you inside a true story of my own where through my eyes and heart, I shared with you the false hopes of my own misunderstandings. **Brain dead** means **not living;** proving to us all that once brain death has occurred, it cannot be reversed.

Questions arose from the very core of my heart; questions that "PROOF" will answer. Where is the life that is in the brain when a person is alive; even if they are in a coma?

"PROOF" searched the minds of the Medical, Biblical, scholars for their answers; from the wise ones of ancient times such as King Solomon to the ones on the internet today. Yes, let the wisdom be collaborated and compiled to hear the truth of this matter, **O.L.B.A.C.**

This must begin at the beginning because everything that has a purpose has a beginning. "Everything or anything that **never** happened or happens; never had or has a **purpose** to happen at all!"

If it never happened, it wasn't meant to. "You can "quote" me on that! What came first; the chicken or the egg? The chicken had to lay the egg, so the chicken came before the egg.

According to Genesis in the old Testament of the King James Version; Every animal was made after its kind male and female, of course they had mates and moving right along to the subject of the egg, that was laid by the female chicken was how the egg was laid and not made by speaking it into existence.

That is the "PROOF that Moses gave in the history book in K.J.V., and you know the Bible wrote that Noah was able to gather the chickens for the ark; but I didn't read any place, yet, where he gathered up eggs to save in the Ark instead of chickens! "PROOF" proves this to be true, with your smiles and nods of approval!

There is a time for everything under the heavens! "PROOF" is a book to arouse you in the way of your conception; cajole your understanding of the knowledge of O.L.B.A.C. Speaking of arousal; this is the very best way to remind you of my book "CAJOLED BY DOPAMINE AT CONCEPTION & BEYOND;" now that book takes you from kisses to conception compared to this book.

"PROOF" will take you right in the very cajoled central nervous systems; with the rushing of blood in their blushing genitals. Their bodies are made for preparing them for the "dance" of love. This male and female really are more than physically attracted to one another; they are "Inlove." I will let "PROOF" narrate how they feel and relate it along with their hypothalamus gland all the way to the very moment of how, where, why, and when, O.L.B.A.C.

I was cajoled to give you "PROOF." I will give you "PROOF." Truth will cajole you as you have never been cajoled by truth before. Just remember, you asked for "PROOF," because you wanted "PROOF," and I was cajoled by dopamine to oblige you.

"PROOF" you shall receive.

CHAPTER 12

THE CON IN CONCEPTION!

OUR LIFE BEGINS at conception repeatedly, in different concepts, in a "Con" and "Cept" way! Excuse my puns here, but "PROOF" must tell the truth just like it is. O.L.B.A.C. is the biggest set up of being "conned" ever known by everyone starting at our own conceptions.

Whether you're talking about our love; life and love go hand in hand, they bond together within and between.

Whether you're talking about our conception; without life there is no conception. Whether you're talking about the brain; without life in the brain, there is no living.

The activity conducted and orchestrated from the hypothalamus gland just the size of an almond secretes the hormones to support life and keep these things healthy and happy; these things must have life to begin and to last! The giver of all things pertaining to life is given by God!

"PROOF" brings to your mind the saying that God has a flower garden; we never heard of God having a weed garden, there are no weeds! The weed of lust is left to wander to wherever it may, but not in the garden. The "flower of Love" is stabilized and is not allowed to wander; planted, cultivated, and carefully attended by the gardener!

There are flowers that only last for a season; but Every flower starts as a flower, never changing to be a weed, but is a flower. Factors of lust include rapid sexual activity that results in S.T.D.'s and production of dysfunctional actions that alter the lives like an invasive vine that choke out the very energy out of our lives!

The "Flower of Love" is tended and cared for by the garner; cultivated and nourished with the continued bathing of the action from the hormones of "Life energy." This lust withers and fades as just a weed; and thrill is nothing but a rush, an imitation of the real thing! A weed is not a flower. "Weeds of lust" emotions that are invasive, aggressive posing the integrity of self-worth and even dominate the wellbeing of a "SOULOVE" begins within the Soul from the very Spirit of God and the "**continual involuntary sparking**" deep within the nucleus of the hypothalamus gland; the gland you can't live without or "SOULOVE" (up to a couple of day)off of just oxygen from life support machines after the brain is dead.

Lust doesn't last very much longer than minute activities from spurts of hormonal excitements; then suddenly as *if* the brain dies, the hypothalamus gland sends no *lasting* energy to support *lust*, it is just a moment of pleasure that soon fades as a weed in the sunset. A little lust only requires a little hormone action, but that little bit of feeling soon stops due to time, chance and changes in life, "PROOF" it's not real life-love!

Our choice is his permissive will to make choices with our 5 senses; a choice gambling with time, chance and change and personal designed disasters! **God's divine will be involuntary**

action according to the Spiritual will of God that can't be controlled by our 5 senses.

This involuntary action that you can't control; the spirit of life's energy is what God has control of through our Hypothalamus Gland. "PROOF" of that is the fact that O.L.B.A.C. and physical attraction can end up in a "**con**cept" of being trapped in a conception regardless of the male and female were "JOINED" by the life-love-energy of God.

Let "PROOF" take you deeper than what never meets the eye; deep skin diving far within the center of the brain of a man and a woman when the very instance they are **"cajoled by dopamine!"** Is it "physical lust" or is it "Spiritual love?" What has God got to do with our hormones and deoxyribonucleic acid? God has a permissive will and a divine will.

PROOF" proves that only God can "join" the man and woman "SPIRITUALLY" together, before the two of them can blink an eye! It takes just 8.2 seconds for a man to fall in love, that's less than 10 seconds! Effectually, the Bible would call that a "rapture" which in that case would happen within a "twinkling of an eye!" "PROOF" can be very simple, but then in this case, it can be very perplexing and complicated and full of **hormonal, sugar phosphates and nitrogen** drama; and to be quite honest with you, love has no other way to rock you with endearment for one person in life, than through the perfect will of God's timing!

It must be understood here and now that there is a "Mystery" in the Divine joining of making a Man one with one Woman;" becoming together spiritually in a new beginning as one in this "INLOVE CONCEPTION!" This "Inlove-Conception" between them has never existed before and does not give them the option to separate themselves ever from this spiritual bond once conception has occurred!

"LIFE-**CONCEPTION" is a CHEMICAL conception THAT TAKES PLACE INSIDE THE SACRED FEMALE**.

This fusing and bonding **in a forever-identity-**Conception between their **D.N.A**; "**One flesh,** becoming that of a child, **from** the two parents of different D.N.A! O.L.B.A.C.

"Life is also the beginning of love; starting from the spark of "life-energy" where it counts most, from within the chemistry between two people!

There is a saying that comes to mind;" It's what's **upfront** that counts." There is an attraction "**upfront**" that goes deeper than what meets the eye, when "what's upfront" makes the difference between lust and **love; and "whether the action is lasting!"**

You just may be surprised what you may learn through PROOFreading That was another pun; but, keep reading "PROOF" and may your heart be enlightened, sparked with knowledge and wisdom!

The King has brought me into his chambers; who is this King? Where is his chambers? The one whom my Soul loveth, the one who has set me as a seal upon his heart!! Let him kiss me with the kisses of his mouth! For your love is better than wine; your love is stronger than death, and hath the most vehement flame The eyes are the windows of the Soul; this is a true saying, but the Soul houses the spirit that rejoices when the ears hears the voice of "My Beloved!"

Ah, the voice of my Beloved; but the magnate within us, draws me after you; let us run. What is this magnate; where is it inside? Love is the magnate, deep within the center of my brain; secreted as a hormone in an involuntary action under the sovereign will of God.

Our life truly does begin at conception; conception of the positive and the negative bonding together with neutrons that had no mass without the life energy, the miracle that is involuntary in the atom of deoxyribonucleic acid! True mates are one of a kind; chosen not by us volunteering, or picking or choosing, but by powers of the positive proton's electro excitable cells and the negative electrons bonding together the zero-charge mass within one Man and one Woman, in a once in a lifetime connection.

This is the true conception between God and "whom" he joins together that "no Man" can separate! Deep within the nucleus of the brain's center called the hypothalamus; a satellite for the body that keeps the body healthy and happy, continues to seek, draw, and cajole only joining the suited of opposites together, (Man & Woman **"WoMan" SPIRITUAL INVOLUNTARY MARRIAGE BOND**) (sperm & egg **"CONCEPTION" INVOLUNTARY BOND OF 46 CHROMOSOMES**) in unity of **O.L.B.A.C. full of hormonal drama!**

Men have been conned by the "pro" abilities of the female ever since the nucleus of the male shaped like a sphere appearing hostile; compared to the female being more elongated and friendly! Even before we were born; our hypothalamus gland was secreting hormones, pre-planned inspirational defense guards for the male to fight his way into areas that of the female.

The hypothalamus gland of a female is different from that of a male; needless for "PROOF" to try to ovoid the fact that many strong men have been brought down by the wrong female according to the bible that refer the woman of **lust** as "the strange woman."

Female is capable to cajole the very life agent from a male; cajoling him to drop his spear; standing commando and surrender to her demands be one flesh within her grasps. All too often through lust of our flesh; (what they see, feel, want and their pride of life which is not love from God's will but of the choices made at the time of chance and the whelms of change) being one is only for one dance of lust and not a dance of love resulting in a life time of love, and breathing our last breath still in love!

Our hypothalamus gland controls our heart in the way that is without our conscience effort to do so; we can attempt to hold our breath as well as take quick breaths on demand, but it's only temporally.

"PROOF" can tell you of children who hold their breath when they don't get what they want and it can be a terrifying experience for a parent; We can choose to set our affection upon whom we so desire to do so; but our senses change without much respect to how we feel about them. Like our breathing; we can lust after what our sensory organs offer us, by trying to hold on to that one look, or sound, or taste or feeling or breath.

We must let the hypothalamus gland decide when we **must** breathe and who we "Soulove." We throw fits of temper tantrums like children; we all do want our own ways to be given to us when it comes to God and his divine control over life, love and Marriage. Crying over what we see and think we should have to keep what we see for ourselves! We want it now, all of it, and we want things done our way! We all are conceived from seeds of the sperm that was selfish, demanding and greedy.

This is the way we are in lust with our eyes and feelings and, we cry like babies wanting what most of the time our parents tell us "no we can't have it!" God is the same way with us as His children; he says no to our feelers called sensory organs until it is with the right person, in the right time, and producing the right things!

"You have eyes, but you see not; you have ears but you hear not, lest at any time you began to see with your eyes (spiritually) and hear with your ears (spiritually) and be converted, you will no wise enter in the wisdom of God to have the peace or love of God that only his will gives. O.L.B.A.C. true knowledge; but life Begins with life, and life begins with the giver of life.

The confusion and woe start with when we try to control what is **involuntar**y action with just our common **voluntary** sensory organs. "PROOF" proves to you that our sensory organs are only good for us to help us get around in this atmosphere which is physical.

Our physical sensory organs were not designed for ex-ray vision, to see things invisible, or even to hear things light-years away, or to feel things before they happen, or to know things about people whether they will be happy with you for a lifetime. "PROOF" proves that some of you have read in the K.J.V. "Your foes are those of your own household; but you thought you could trust your heart, when the K.J.V. wrote to us saying, the heart was wicked and who can know it?

Our purpose for our physical 5 senses is to manage getting around physically on earth, but these sensory organs alone would not help us on the moon without a spacesuit and shuttle! Using our 5 sensory organs; medically called the sense organs - eyes, ears, tongue, skin, and nose- help to protect the body we must use at our own control to get around, cook, and eat to keep our body healthy. These sensory organs just like the houses we live in which are not in any way "spiritual or involuntary!

These voluntary senses are just conventional means that have their limited abilities most of the time and cannot be dependent upon to work or even to last. We can voluntarily decide to make our bodies do things; sit, stand, walk, jump, run, E.T.C. the sensory organs cannot be dependent upon to put much trust in them.

"PROOF" will tell you that in the pursuit from the enemy, a granddaddy (Opiliones) long leg can voluntarily tear off one section of a leg joint; throw it in the direction of the enemy as a plea-bargain in hopes this will distract the enemy allowing his escape! We (are not classified as Arachnids) don't grow other limbs, by any actions of our abilities!

We don't have the choice or the power to voluntarily become benevolent fictional characters with superhuman powers with strength and abilities to run as fast as a locomotive-engine; faster than a speeding-metal-bullet or by no means fly and flock like any given choice bird of feathers.

"PROOF" proves the involuntary action will allow one to do the supernatural! With that knowledge; "PROOF" will prove with understanding why your involuntary action does not allow you to choose those actions, or the right to use them when you want. We try to have our way, sometimes, but our involuntary actions are not made to be used, without major consequences for trying.

The involuntary action serves with the goal for life-love-conceptions; however, and sadly to say our voluntary action's run horrible interferences with just trying to walk around. Our common everyday walk around sense is often not to be trusted. Our voluntary action is just sensory action suitable for our change of mind. "PROOF" dug out this saying; today chickens, tomorrow feathers! K.J.V. "if it be God's will, we will do this or that."

The question "PROOF" will ask you as the reader; how does God **give** us a mate? "PROOF" will answer your question in one word. **INVOLUNTARLY!**

You were conceived Involuntarily, given love involuntarily and you die involuntarily. Involuntary action is all God's will! "In God do we live, move and have our being." K.J.V.

"PROOF" is aware of the 6th sense; and this sense is what is used for spiritual guidance in spiritual things not seen, heard, felt or in any of the common 5 sensory organs. "PROOF" is telling you that we have meat, dairy, fruits, vegetables, and fish that are the basic food category that supply our physical needs that we must consume daily voluntarily.

Using our 5 sensory organs; medically called the sense organs - eyes, ears, tongue, skin, and nose- help to protect the body we must use at our own control to get around, cook, and eat to keep our body healthy. These sensory organs just like the atmosphere we live in are not in any way "spiritual or involuntary!

Many Bible Scholars are aware of the verse that reads "When a man finds a wife; he shall then leave his father and Mother and cleave to his wife and they shall be "**one flesh**." "PROOF" must prove that the simple truth has been **physically misunderstood**!

"One flesh" had nothing to do with anything other than in the ultimate event of them having a child that sealed their D.N.A. together as one (a new life.) How many times have you had a conception with a different partner? Each partner caused you to become one flesh together for as long as that child lives!

The other word that "PROOF" will prove is the understanding of the word "JOINED." The law is of the people. By the people and for the people; the law marriage license is just a paper signed that can be voided that same day!

Each person is asked this question "do," or "will" they "TAKE" the other person to" BE" theirs lawfully! There is "PROOF" that some refused to "take", and they left smiling; but "PROOF" proves that there has been a thin line between "stealing and "taking" in the eyes of God. When you promise to love when God hasn't given it to the both of you, it's called trespassing against God!'

God is not a "LAW" God is "SPIRIT." God does not ask a man and woman anything…. God just "JOINS" them by his spirit. They are already spiritually and are married by God's s spiritual rights which is above the laws of the people! The hypothalamus gland takes direct orders from God that gives us Life, Soulove, and without restriction of your voluntary actions of your 5 sensory organs!

"PROOF" takes pride in this scripture from the King's version; you did not choose God, but God chose you, before the foundations of the world began. "PROOF" will allow you to tear that page out of the Bible.

"PROOF" proves God chose you, God knew you before you were born, before you were even in your mother's womb. God knew us all when we were naked quarks (spirit) without a positive proton to bond with.

God controls the hypothalamus! The hypothalamus is not deceived by our sensory organs; that is constantly changing and as the hormones give us pleasure that often leave us in situations that send more messages to the hypothalamus gland that send our blood pressure racing and our emotions on a roller coaster ride soon to crash in an event of a unplanned parenthood. O.L.B.A.C.

"PROOF" will prove to you by your own words that there is a way that right unto us all, but the ends there of are not so pleasant. You have your choice to use your body's sensory organs to assume love; but it will be like being on "life support machines" while being comatose. Your emotion God will permit you to become one flesh with 50 different people; making babies and never have the spirit of God joining you with none of them!

"PROOF" will tell you that being "ONE FLESH" will never join you by God's spirit with anyone. You can be "joined" by God's spirit of love and may never be "ONE FLESH." One flesh simply means to conceive a child **with** someone.

Becoming one flesh is still the same whether God joined the happy parents in 'Love", or in some cases, that can be no more than what you call an accidental or unplanned conception, a child support case and a need for a babysitter.

When you make a baby, you are one flesh period with that person for as long as that baby lives! You can and will be not more joined by the D.N.A. of the other parent than if you never met them; ever!

O.L.B.A.C. is such a big subject; but conception between a man and his (A) woman is what starts it all! I'm really trying very hard to get the intimacy going; but there's a lot to be said in the meantime. Conception between a man and "HIS" Chosen wife, by God makes her different from that of any other female; ever! What is that difference?

I once asked my God given husband if I were his woman. He was quiet for a few seconds. His answer surprised me. He said "a woman can give pleasure to a man for one night; she is his woman for that night, but tomorrow night, she will be a woman to some other man. She will be a woman to any man who gives her two senses from his sensory organs for her services;" the pun is too much like truth here!

His voice began to touch me with his passion of love mixed with wisdom and tenderness; he continued to speak saying, "if *you* were walking down the street; everyone man would say, you are a "woman, walking down the street; but when *I* see you walking down the street, I would say *you are my wife!*" My Chosen, My Beloved knows who I am by the spirit of Love that joined us together for as long as we both shall breathe. We shall love one another! Indivisible, Unconditional Love.

Only God gives a man a wife; the law just asks you will you just take her! When God gives a man a wife; she belongs to only him! There will be no mistaking when God gives you breath without thinking; and when God involuntarily gives a man a wife without him thinking to ask for her!

The sensory gland of my ears instantly adjusted to the voice on the other end of the line; without even a blink of my eye, I became aware of a man's voice entwined with happiness! A joy that I had never experienced before other than acquainting it to the divine Love of God! Inside my brain was God taking control of my life without my thinking.

Who ever said that "Love is blind" understood how the hypothalamus gland works weeding out faults that the sensory organs point out as surface pleasures of lust that only last tempera-rely! God tends the garden of our life separating the lust from love! Our Hypothalamus Gland must be the "GARDEN OF LIFE-& LOVE." For sure we are put out of the garden of life; and it is guarded by the Arch Angels holding flames of fire.

The hypothalamus is hooked up to God; It keeps me breathing even when I'm asleep. Furthermore, we are as in a "brain-fog" when it comes to finding the right person to love without out God connecting us with the right one.

When the hypothalamus detects the right voice; suddenly it secretes dopamine that are released on a level that remembers to give that good feeling, that reward when we meet the right one for life!

When I heard my Beloved voice, instantly, there was a joy that has never gone away! He experienced the same effects with my voice and his hypothalamus gland! Sex had nothing to do with this joining of God! The voice was used to as the only contact between us' our voices can't be seen or felt; yet the hypothalamus did what was the first "conception" between us as chosen by God. This is a true Spiritual joining of the Spirit of God that no man can separate us from.

There is the other kind of love that is built upon the physical attraction only. We know that "PROOF" must prove truth. Truth is that knowledge that is true! There is no other way to tell the truth other than the life of the body.

The bible reads that the life of the body is in the blood; however, when it comes down to drinking blood in the bible with Jesus, that's a different story and subject. The medical, science and biology will tell us that there is a universal blood that you all can receive; but that blood type being O-blood type cannot receive any other blood type but O- or O+!

God has made mates the same way! We have the silly mindsets that being in-love with someone was liking the favorite movies or colors or popcorn? Being in-love is a spiritual God Blessing that is "given" only by God to a man; and not "given or taken by any law of man!" Moses made a true mistake trying to make what only God does with marriage and suggested "divorce; we all began to be smitten as hardheaded rocks and look what happened to Moses when he failed to obey God and smote the rock!

I know you really think "PROOF went off the deep edge here but proving the K.J.V. refers us as not only hardheaded, but stiff-necked (stupid) rebellious, and stony-hearted rocks! Let me quickly get that proven down to the scripture Deuteronomy 31:27

The greatest gift known to man is favor given to him in the form of a "Wife", not a girlfriend. Love begins at conception, first between only God and those he joins; then from that union is the conception of their bodies, and that concludes WHERE O.L.B.A.C.!

Where does the woman of a man's love come from? His Soul! So why would you try to look for her drinking in a club? "PROOF" will prove that you give strong drink to those that are ready to parish; and K.J.V. wrote that too! Why would you think you should trust any of your five senses when they are cursed with a curse of changes and failure?

The hypothalamus gland is designed to work under God's control who gives life, love and Blessings; "PROOF" must tell you that everybody doesn't have blessings from God! You are blessed to be born; But according to the bible, "children are the blessings of God and these blessings make you rich and add no sorrow unto you. Let's all count ourselves as blessings each with a name, one by one, let's start with our own life as a blessing from God! O.L.B.A.C.

Whether you were blessed by God to be joined by his spiritual love from the Soul; or you were caught up in the snare of your 5 senses and now you lay skin to skin together, the bodies of both male and females have differences that are meant to come together. Behind the whole process; the hypothalamus has been busy as usual, but let's take a medical look at what's going on inside the males' point of view.

It was a normal day for the male; the hypothalamus was keeping the blood pressure 120/80, not bad for a male at the age of over 21, but let's give this male more maturity. This male is not a boy that is still trying to grow a few hairs on his chin; the hypothalamus has long sent out messages awakening the pituitary gland to kick in his testosterone.

This male is a senior citizen that has retired and is still very much a man in all rights. He likes his face clean shaven; seduced with only a hint of aftershave splashed on his smooth unblemished skin. The hypothalamus gland secreted messages from the sensory organs has pretty much kept his sexual life to zero.

Life is all about others until you're "INLOVE," then suddenly, it's no more me, but we. Love is not about the world around you, not even your favorite color or food; it's about one male and one woman.

Of course his sleep has been disturbed; sex hormones released from his dopamine that reward him for the pleasure of being with skin to skin with a woman that returns pleasure for pleasure from "Soulove" God has not touched his life in that manner….yet!

The hypothalamus gland is treating this senior male like he is "Soulove-desensitized." A person that is "brain-fogged;" as long as the oxygen is given, he goes on appearing to be living, but with no "Soulove" he is living, but desensitized inside!

What is the male's hypothalamus doing just now when he is desensitized to love? Remember the hypothalamus gland is vital for the health and happiness of the body. "PROOF" proves the very core of one's faith to be not tested; but proven in this life-energy!

Life-energy provoking the very essence of Medical evidence bewitched at diabolical timing; modern day Biblical believers are yet baffled and amazed by the fact that life's invisible energy that sparks from quarks (sparks.) The smallest particles building substances that are impossible to not only to be seen, but they are extremely difficult to measure within the makeup in the proton and electron.

Confounded we are and shall continue to be; "Life-energy is invincible, invisibly-insensible, unbridled and absolutely-+ positively, the very solvent will of God! The Bible reads that it is not good for man to be alone. God designed the help mate that was never to be found except by the leading of the invisible forces within the man that will direct and connect to the right woman.

The chosen woman; one that was (altered to be neutral, agreeable to Adam the first man and this is the way it stands for every man that is given a Godly mate, he must be led by the spirit of God, which is life; God is love, God is life, without God there is no love or life.) with more than just skin; but God connected the energy of the cellular-proton, electron-reactive-**bond; "sealing them in**

an invincible, invisibly-insensible, unbridled absolutely positive love!"

Only God can join a Man to one woman in the connection called "LOVE" that lasts for as long as they both shall breathe! Adam was given a mate; he was not a boy; but a man that knew God joined him together with a "chosen mate!" God does not ask us to take a mate; the involuntary will of God like your puberty, is involuntary and freely given in a precise timing.

However, because we have changed and digressed from God's spiritual laws, we cannot change God, God changes things, because God does not change! Moses in the Bible offered then as it still stands today an imitation life support machine for people who God did not join by Love.

The law is for the ones that "take" unto themselves what only a law, made by Moses and public acceptance to trespass (possession is 9/10ᵗʰ. Of the law)) against another person's mate before God's will, and a paper signed with ink of the deed committed!! God's will does not change; but heaven (your mind) and earth (your body) will pass away as "PROOF" proves when our sensual vows, and the very health of our bodies presenting itself as a key witness from the hypothalamus's involuntary evidence of our consensual-common-walk-a-round-lifestyles!

CHAPTER 13

COMMAND CONNECTION

"PROOF" WILL TAKE you right to the heart of the matter; where there is no love in life, there is no home in the house! The hypothalamus gland has been sending out SOS signals to the male for sometime now. The whole body feels out of whack; allergies pop up uninvited disrupting sleep as well as often as routine and considered just something that is normal for this male. What has the hypothalamus gland got to do with this love deprived male?

"PROOF" is so glad you are asking a question that will be more than answered. The hypothalamus has already been aware of this deprivation long before any symptoms like recklessness, early awakening, fatigue, and the list goes on! Ongoing loneliness can affect even the most seemingly outgoing person. Being the "life of the party" doesn't necessarily exclude someone from being chronically lonely. This type of loneliness can eventually impact all areas of your life.

Inability to connect with others on a deeper, more intimate level. Maybe you have friends and family in your life, but engagement with them is at a very surface level. Your interaction doesn't feel connected in a way that is fulfilling and this disconnection seems never ending. "NO CLOSE OR "BEST" FRIENDS.

You have friends, but they are casual friends or acquaintances and you feel you can find no one who truly "gets" you. This is a loneliness that makes you feel isolated, yes you may be surrounded by dozens of people, yet you it's as if you're in your own unbreakable bubble. These feelings --long-term--are another possible symptom of chronic loneliness.

The hypothalamus is feeling all this pressure as it has raised the amount of blood pressure to make up for the stress from lack of sleep. The cortisol levels go up; a stress hormone sent from the hypothalamus gland which can impair cognitive performance, compromise the immune system, and increase your risk for vascular problems, inflammation and heart disease.

It is not good to be alone; or feeling unloved. You are 50% more likely to die prematurely from being unloved and lonely than those with healthy social relationships. Loneliness is as lethal as smoking 15 cigarettes per day!

Those that come into the hospital for chronic issues, such as back pain and breathing difficulties, Patients who lived alone or were felt disconnected at home were often suffering rejection and or just unloved. Elderly people who want companionship yet even though those around don't reach out to you only makes your thalamus gland reduce your immunity, which can increase your risk of disease. It also increases inflammation in the body, which can contribute to heart disease and other chronic conditions.

Marriage in most societies, is considered a permanent social and legal contract and a relationship between two people that is based on mutual rights and obligations among the spouses. This conception is often based on a romantic, relationship, though this is not always the case. Let's go inside this male body; and let's give this male a name. "PROOF" will wrap this book around him and the time for love!

This man's name is just fitting for who he is to the woman; he is simply the other half of woman, but he is 100% "MAN." "PROOF" honors every male for being what God called him from the beginning; and in this truth rest the name of this male to be called "Mann!"

Mann and Wo were destined to come together in the very will of God! The instant the phone was handed to Wo and before she could say "hello; within a twinkling of their eye," **God had willed HIS INVOLUNTARY HORMONAL ACTION IN <u>AN</u> "COMMAND CONNECTION!"**

I pounder here; realizing that life will never be the same after this couple hears the others voice for the very first time! "PROOF" must get it all down pat; everything must be told in detail, as the cell phone rings! It has been a long day and the evening was drawing the shadows of his eyelids over his eyes as he wondered what his friend would be up to as he eyed the caller's name and I.D. on his cell phone.

This is a time for love; Mann hears his cell phone ringing. The sensory organs on the outside of Mann's head is directing the sound to the reaches of the cochlea, tiny hair cells known as stereocilia react to the sound vibrations and transmit them into electrical signals captured by the auditory nerve. At this point Mann is not in control of what is going on inside his head!

"PROOF" will prove to you how the hypothalamus gland, the small almond sized portion in the center of his brain that suddenly takes mind that is over matter kicking out an involuntary action just as the male cradles his cell phone close to his head.

The hypothalamus gland stood by monitoring the homeostatic of Mann's body; all is calm. Just picture his blood pressure at this moment; 120/80, not bad for a man retired. His patience is relaxed as he leans his back up comfortably against the back of his lazy boy chair, resting his elbow on the edge of his computer desk.

all is well as the two friends chatted back and forth. Of course, Mann's brain translated the impulses of his friend's voice into a familiar one he knew; while the hypothalamus gland rewarded them both with the happy hormone called dopamine.

The laughter and smiles shared between old memories began to fade into a relaxed mode as the two men reminisced over the years. As a last minute's jester, the Friend smiled over to his right side of the table sitting beside him at this woman eating and spoke to Mann; "Hey Man," the friend suddenly said, "I want you to meet someone."

Mann waited on his end of the distance between them; like a blind man, of course Mann didn't know who it was that his friend wanted him to say hello to. While his Friend took the chance to catch off guard the woman next to him, handed his cell phone to her. They are just platonic friends eating a quick meal after bumping into each other.

The power of suggestion; and the element of surprise! This law of attraction; no, it does not have a hourglass shape, but here "PROOF" will translate this image to your mind's eye as the hypothalamus gland casting soft incandescent light; waiting for the sensory organs between a male and female to speak to each other, as they each hear a voice that will affect them like none other voice ever heard!

The hypothalamus is not only a heart regulator; the hypothalamus gland controls the pituitary gland that holds Oxycontin; the love hormone! Of course, we have no control over our involuntary action of our brain, over our hypothalamus gland any more than Mann, hearing the voice on the other end of the receiver say "HELLO___ HOW ARE YOU DOING___Mann?"

The hypothalamus of Mann responded to the sound of this voice by releasing a chemical hormone called dopamine; an electrical neurotransmitter traveling through Mann's central nervous center sending Mann a spark that instantly overwhelmed him with indescribably joy! This was beyond anything Mann had ever felt in his life.

Mann sat stunned by this power of joy that came as a direct conman connection with a woman he knew nothing of, or about other than he Loved her at the very first sound of her voice! The hypothalamus is controlled by the unseen hand of God; we live and breathe and have our being, and who we Soulove is chosen involuntarily by God just like our heartbeat!

Mann's hypothalamus gland made him feel happy and kept him happy involuntary when it kicks out those happy hormones flowing throughout his central nervous system. It was an all body experience that left Mann totally changed from the stimulus of the hypothalamus.

Mann did not mention anything to what he was feeling to the woman on the cell whom he never met physically; how could he explain what he was feeling when he had no idea what was happening. He recalled exchanging how pleased he was to have spoken to this woman while trying to keep his voice normal.

The hypothalamus gland was not only working at lightning speeds with Mann; but on the other person on the cell phone, the woman was much elated when she heard the voice of Mann. This is truly the way she would explain what happened to her.

There is a time for love. We will give this woman a name also; "Wo!" Her name shall be called Wo; because she is the "other half" of Mann! "PROOF" makes no mistake with the name of the perfecting of couples meant to be together that God joins spiritually! They are the other half of themselves. O.L.B.A.C. with the egg and the sperm; having the 23 chromosomes of the other half of that when united will become one whole conception, which is 46 chromosomes together!

"PROOF" proves that life and love has a conception beginning with the 1 in a 6, billion, 950 million, 678 thousand, and 119 people; only 1 will be chosen in a life-love conception between a male and 1 woman.

Little can Wo justify what she is feeling! She too is being cajoled by her dopamine; as the deep stirring male voice by the man that was simply saying "hello Wo, how are you?" Suddenly became her sunshine that light up her very soul! She had no time to think, it just happened the very instance she heard his voice.

Male and female were destined to come together in the very will of God! The instant the phone was handed to her, and before she could say "hello; within a twinkling of their eye," **God had willed HIS INVOLUNTARY HORMONAL ACTION IN <u>AN</u> "COMMAND CONNECTION!"**

Let "PROOF" elaborate here that when the hypothalamus gland sends chemical hormones throughout the bloodstream and into the central nervous system; that does not mean what you feel, someone else feels it also. that is your hypothalamus gland working in you. Also, just because you feel sparks from dopamine; does not mean that it will continue to keep you feeling it, it may be no longer than an elevator ride, or the event equal to that of a roller coaster ride that you threw up and had a bad memory of that you recall every time you think of a roller coaster!

"PROOF" will tell you we all have electrical censors charging hormones through us; as we voluntarily use our common 5 senses making everything even marriage, intimacy and family just a **common everyday hormonal thing**. With involuntary H.G. actions keep us healthy as well as protecting us from emotionally damaging weak unbridled lust by controlling the happy feelings; and saving the best for a **once in a lifetime lasting connection** to our one and only "other half."

There were times in the past when people lived in villages and hunted for food walking for miles. One of their instincts was to feel the chemical reaction of their body reacting with the stranger; if they gave you a positive reaction of no threat, then they would be treated as friend or even family.

"PROOF" proves that chemistry between someone may be of many things you have in common with someone, not always a good thing in the long run. Most of the time you are just feeling the red light of someone to avoid in life-love.

Wo has long since hung up with Mann after each of them being cajoled by the hand of God in the involuntary action of the hypothalamus gland in a way that only can happen by God! "PROOF" has proven that not only do we need the hypothalamus gland to live; but this gland emits messages into the central nervous system from every sound, everything we put in our mouth, and what we feel and what we smell and at the instance of whom we meet.

It is only God who chooses whether we are joined with someone ("in-love") or just emotional "in-lust." "PROOF" will prove to you that a flower of love just in the bud; a beautiful rose was about to bloom in the garden of love between Mann and Wo. The hypothalamus gland is happy sending out love notes between them.

The difference between being in-love and in-lust with someone is simple. Love doesn't change; it grows with you! Love is involuntary spiritual action that you can't make, stop, or give it away, this spirit is not ours to give to anyone. Love is a gift of the spirit of God. The love between Mann and Wo is the true joining of life-energy between a man and 1 woman (marriage). However, with lust; it only begins with our 5 senses and those things change like the weather, from one person to the other.

To be in "Lust" can be with anyone or groups of persons places or things and even with just one's self; all at the same time even. People can have a lust for an Actress or Actor, Sport-Hero or some other famous persons, but that's not the kind of chemistry that would join you as one. Only God can join just one man with just one woman with love for as long as they both shall breathe!

"PROOF" now demonstrates just how easy it is to think you are in love with someone when it's just your sensory organs dancing with your hormones, but give yourself chance to simmer down with that

H.G., because if it is true love, you will have more than just a feeling; you "**have a gift of God**" <u>together</u>!!

There is so much to be said here; but to put it in a short way, the difference the hypothalamus makes here with Mann and Wo is that they have more going on between them than what meets their 5 senses! They have never met. They have never touched. They only heard each other's voices; and with the very first word, "hello" the hypothalamus gland did something that was an involuntary action!

It's not rare for people to get together as strangers set up a blind date by a friend that knows them both. The phone and dopamine start making one or even both people feel pleasure from the thoughts of meeting. The seduction of the central nervous system cajoles one or both to daydream and fantasize. This is making you understand the common grounds between us all when we let our 5 senses seduce us along with the help of hormones.

It's just a game and a walk in the park of catering to our random hormones secreted by the hypothalamus gland; while our heart is steadily beating, and our breath is being directed by this small gland and the right hand of the unseen hand of God.

So many people commonly became intimate just because they felt happy when someone smiled or spoke softly or went to school together, worked together or went to the same Church to meet God! What insult to injury can "PROOF" add to the fire of life woes as you partied together, and the hypothalamus gland began loading your blood stream with other hormones like Oxycontin that made you want to cuddle?

How can you resist when serotonin is added to the game of chance and change and what is a party without drugs and music! Everyone plays the fool to their 5 senses looking for love in all the wrong places. Self-control is just a caution that is tossed aside the more fun you have, the less mental is used!

Endorphin begin kicking you into overdrive and before you know it; the hypothalamus gland stops the flow of hormones, and the happy feeling goes away. When this gland acts normally; everybody feels dopamine, oxytocin, serotonin and endorphin from time to time, whether they make you feel happy or angry, but they don't stick around very long when all they must go by is your 5 senses!(now you see it, now you don't)

"PROOF" proves your 5 senses are controlled by you and the changes around your life. You lust after what you can never be satisfied over even if you had it, you lose interest with it! Mann & Wo are different! From now on the **hypothalamus gland referred to in this book a.k.a. H.G.**

Let's keep it real; "PROOF" knows that the H.G. can stabilize your equilibrium; but it can make you giddy when you feel all that happiness flowing in your body such as both Mann and Wo were. Keep in mind that neither the two of them know what the other is feeling and their feelings did not go away, even when they lived miles and miles apart and never spoke of this joy between them as years passed! "Life-Love" is an energy that changes not! Gravity cannot give it it's movement. Time, demons, weather, distance or anything you can think of is greater than love.

Nothing can separate Mann from Wo once the energy of life-love connects them. There is a magnate drawing them together just like the sperm and the egg within them; the chemistry is already drawing them together for their conception, but it's a long way to go and only one can be chosen. Just one man and 1 woman. One sperm and one egg. One baby through one birth at a time. Even in the birth of twins; one is born at a time! "PROOF" will not be stumped; just one at a time!

"PROOF" goes beyond the 5 senses; understanding the H.G. continues to send out the happy hormones; as sparks of energy activated once Mann and Wo first heard each other's voice. H.C. works in this fashion as when the blood pressure elevates to a higher level. When two people are "In-Love" together the two experience a unique sensation that only happens when their spirits have been bonded by the act of God, not just emotions and voluntary choices of their own choosing.

You can choose to be in lust with someone, but you cannot choose whom "God joins you with in love;" you cannot alter, stop, or change God's will! You can choose to involuntary hold your breath; but the involuntary action of the H.G. will not be bullied, by your choice of volunteerism.

Can this be proven that the H.G. levels can determine if a male and female are in-love with each other or just temporally stimulated by their H.G.? "PROOF" has the answer. Just like the heart can only beat for so long when the brain is dead; lust or infatuation can only last so long as the sensory organs send messages to the H.G.

The H.G. responds by rewarding the body with the feel-good hormones; but we all know everything changes, and that change alters how we feel, and the brain responds with the response. It's one thing to smile with your face; but love gives you a smile that starts inside; love makes you "smileinsideout for life!

To be in-love together for life with someone take an involuntarily action like only God can order the H.G. to do! Mann and Wo have that gift from God; they don't know that the other is feeling the same thing because they are trying to deny what's happening to them themselves. They are not aware that together they feel the very same **spirit** within that they have known **only** with **God**!

Mann and Wo are destined to be together by the divine will of God that made them. Everything has a purpose under the sun the wise King Solomon wrote; and God has a fail proof plan when He joins a man with one woman; nothing will separate them from that Love! There is something within each of us that defies our own voluntary action; that something is a H.G.

"PROOF" has proven that our very own health and happiness deepens upon the little almond sized shape in the middle of our brains that is shaped differently in a male than in a female, but it was made to come together in time when the H.G. will cajole the right 23 chromosome together like a magnate when God Joins them.

In the meanwhile; we meet up with Mann and Wo as 4 years have passed. The two only talked over the phone, yet neither has ever spoke to reveal their feelings for the other. Very unlike most people that would have taken off like a kite on a windy day.

God is the master mind at work and the two are very much in control of their 5 senses even though they smileinsideout, neither of them can see these smile. The glow of pure joy wherever they go in their separated States and miles and miles away from each other; yet they can feel each other's presence!

The job of the H.G. is truthfully that of a mastermind; our bodies speaks the truth, it asks for what it wants, and if it is God's will and compliant with that will of God, then our body will continue to function at peak levels, supporting our needs of our mission and giving us the sincere desires of our heart.

If you deny your body adequate rest fortifying foods energizing and restorative movement, pleasure, and good company, your hormones will hi jack your mood, energy levels and your metabolism and your H.G. will be forced to possibly shut down to a state of diseases and that's not good for your lust or love life!

H.G. secreting the will of romance between Mann and Wo; even though they have kept this "joy" a secret from the other, this is the very essence of "love" that lovers fight armies, swim oceans, or walk hundredths of miles to be together. Against love, "PROOF" proves, and the Bible is persuaded that there is no law against "love" writes the King James Bible; what shall separate us from the love of God? Nothing shall be against "Love!"

In other words; Mann and Wo are high. Imaging studies confirm new lovers have high amounts of activity in the ventral tegmental area; broadly, the limbic system nuclei include the hypothalamus gland. The part of their brain's reward circuit creates a chemical cocktail giving them intense pleasure and comfort.

They feel obsessed with each other! "PROOF" proves MRI' show that an area of the brain known as the pleasure center lights up when someone thinks of their lover in a way that just doesn't when they think of a friend.

Mann had plenty of common -walk-a-round sense; but the more he tried to make good common sense of what he felt, the more he realized this had nothing to do with his 5 senses any more than it did in the very first time he heard Wo's voice.

The more he tried to deny it; the more he knew it was no use, he loved Wo. He knew how he felt within his Soul; but he also knew that God had given him the most precious gift that a man could receive, and that is his spiritual mate.

Mann knew that he must wait to talk to Wo about their connection; but until the right time came, they would enjoy the joy of love that was warm and glowing in every day all day and through every night within them.

Wo never once hinted about that happiness she feels for Mann inside; "in-love" with one another as 4 1/2 years have passed and all they have done was talked about the climate changes and how each other's family was doing, and the call would be over.

Neither one of them would speak of the effect they heard in their tone of voice; the desires to talk long hours together, and the easy way of laughter between them would be contagious. Wo never once thought of what she felt or even label this joy; she was content to just feel the warmth and the sheer delight in the morning and all day long as she thought of Mann and smileinsideout!

She hardly knew the man that gave her his phone other than seeing him in a Church gathering. H.G. wasted no time matching her up with the joy of a lifetime; but at this point she wasn't to feel guilty of something she had no control over. God was controlling her life! Wo was aware of the dangers of plain emotion that is no deeper than physical attraction; she knew that what was happening was deeper than just physical.

She had the same spiritual awareness that she knew only with the spirit of God! Joy! Wo felt joy connecting her to Mann, but she just knew Mann was not aware of it as far as she was concerned. It takes God to give the spark of life, when O.L.B.A.C. and only God gives the spark that ignites one man with one woman for life; and of course, that spark has already been kindled between Mann and Wo.

Things would have gone on like this for ever; but one day the time came for the budding flower of love to open, Mann held his joy for every conversation every day, but not this day. Many waters cannot quench love, neither can the floods drown it; if a man would give all the substance of his house for love, it would utterly be condemned K.J.V.

No matter what you may think, you may have your opinion, but you are wrong if you think you love with your heart. You love from the depths of your H.G!

It was a beautiful spring day as the tulips and daffodils splashed yellow and red ribbons decorating the green grass displayed in the neighboring manicured yards; Wo listened to the voice feeling her heart dance to every sound that escaped out of his vocal cords. Mann was a kind of man that never trusted anyone with his emotions at heart; and this woman not only had his heart, but she had his "Soul," and there was no letting go because they were Inlove together.

H.G. had been molding their hearts around each other for over 4 years now; but how could they not talk about this love, what would stop them? God truthfully has a divine will in life as we are guided by his involuntary actions within us. Mann knew that he loved Wo, as God had a timely purpose in time that joined them in-love and allow them to become acquainted with each other on an involuntary spiritual level.

Trying to be casual friends with each other is not the way God planned them to be. God made them to be more than just friends when he joined then in the spirit of love the second Mann heard Wo's voice say that first hello! but that is a secret kept between just God and Mann for the time being.

One spring day Mann told Wo that they had a very close connection between them, and this is what made it so easy to talk and understand each other. Of course, Wo listened to Mann as she thought of how she felt about him all these years, but never would she allow herself to make herself appear to suggest she had feelings for anyone that never did so first to her. She knew the two got along so well, they felt the same things right from their very" <u>SPIRITUALLY</u> **involuntary cajoled by dopamine beginning**."

Never was life so wonderful; the two began to express their joy in each other as they seemed like teenagers in-love! Everything was new as the songs seemed to play relating to them as the H.G. danced hormones in their blood stream and into their central nervous systems!

All was well, but they still have never met; the best was yet to come! They didn't know what the other looked like, or anything about the physical appearances of the other one!

But whomsoever God hath joined, let no man separate! The best part of life is knowing God made us unique and wonderfully made! The H.G. is a part of the brain; there is differences between the male and female H.G. and so it was with Wo and Mann's!

Just consider all this information "PROOF" has given you as all part of the "sparking" process; the H.G. has a big job that is very important to the whole life of the male and female to be different and know why there is a difference between their hypothalamus gland right from the nuclei.

"PROOF" needs you to see life-love working not from the outside in; but from the inside out. The love for life must start from the inside; because our conceptions began there within the fallopian tubes of the female, where the same hormonal chemistry of warmth and drawing cajoles the male's sex cell to the egg. Closer, closing the last division of separation between them into being finally one. It's all about life; it's all about conception, it's about that zero hour of connection called love!

The H.G. was made to accommodate the challenges of getting the process done; it will take years to get the couple together, and then years to bring the bodies together and the war between the sperm living up to 5 days, and the egg can't wait no longer than 24 hours.

The vision of the H.G. is well planned and calculated down to a science and to the very second to splitting and dividing cells in the golden silence of time. Only the best will be chosen; the only one chosen will be the best there is for life-love. One man chosen for one woman, one egg chosen for one sperm, one conception one life; Just one!

The volume of a specific nucleus in the H.G. (third cell group of the interstitial nuclei of the anterior hypothalamus) is twice as large in heterosexual men as in women and homosexual men. In addition, the preoptic area that regulates mating behavior, is about 2.2 times larger in men than in women and contains 2 times more cells.

This large size depends on the amount of male sex hormones or androgens. The difference in the area is only apparent after a child is at 4 years old. In girls at 4 years of age there is a decrease in the number of cells in this nucleus. The shape of the suprachiasmatic, involved with circadian rhythms and reproduction cycles is different in men and women.

In males, this nucleus is shaped like a sphere whereas in females it is more elongated. The volume is similar. The difference in shape may be due to different connections. In men, the H.G. has a higher number of androgen receptors (AR) than young adult women.

There are differences in ARs in horizontal diagonal band of Broca, the sexually dimorphic nucleus of the preoptic area, the medial preoptic area, dorsal and ventral area of the periventricular nucleus, the paraventricular nucleus, the supraoptic nucleus, the ventromedial hypothalamus nucleus and the infundibiular nucleus.

Males and females respond differently to ovarian steroids due to differences in estrogen receptor status. The mammillary body complex is known to receive input from the hypothalamus by the fornix. It is involved in cognitive skills. This is different in the two sexes.

These cognitive attributes are different in males and females. Generally, females show advantages in verbal fluency, perceptual speed, accuracy and fine motor skills, while males outperform females in spatial, working memory and mathematical abilities.

"PROOF" concludes research found that men tend to use one side of their brain (particularly the left side for verbal reasoning) while women tend to use both cerebral areas for visual, verbal and emotional responses. These differences in brain use cause a difference in behavior between Mann and Wo.

The differences also bring about several functional differences between males and females. "PROOF" proves for instance, males in most of the species of animals prefer the odor and appearance of females over males. If the sexually dimorphic nucleus of the hypothalamus gland is damaged, this preference for females by males diminishes.

"PROOF" is amazing you with things you never thought about, now can you understand how God has planned a divine will to prove to Mann and Wo that their denial and their choices had nothing to do with the will of God in this wonderful New Day that God has made for them! I am still enjoying coffee and enjoying the events of how "PROOF" proves even the small details in a medically and biblical way that shines a light on the activity of our hypothalamus gland.

Since the death of her last husband; she has been very careful in her preoccupation of where she goes and the type of activities she attends. She gets very lonesome from time to time however; she stays busy with the normal things just like we all do. The day she spoke to Mann over the phone of a mutual friend was purely something that caught her off guard

Wo being a very passionate woman would be to say the very least about her. She loves to feel the real simple pleasures in life; the breezes flowing through the tree that cradles a nest of birds chirping. Breezes blowing the leaves gently as one breaks away and tumbles, resting on the soft blades of green grass beside the bed of her veggie garden. Her natural hair falling over her shoulders and caressing her back with a hint of a cowlick that she sweeps to one side to enhance her feminized beauty; which is nothing more than birthright vain glory.

She thinks of Mann, her Soul can always feel a warmth of a glow inside her that has never gone away since she first heard his voice. Who would have thought that Mann would feel this way, she smiled to herself while floating mentally around the kitchen?

Not every woman is whole; not every woman grows into maturity without the hindrance of the ill effects of drugs. Chickens will not come home to roost if your hormones and metabolism is hi jacked. Being mature in body and mind comes from a happy H.G.

"PROOF" will tell you the truth that age is truly just a number; but love is the true fountain of youth. Love is not blind; but love only has eyes for the one that it is in.

Wo does know this joy she feels when she hears Mann's voice is more than she ever imagined! Wo has a smile that is beginning to be questioned by her family as she has been asked several times lately "what have you been up to lately Wo, with that chest cat smile all over your face?" "Oh!" she replied; trying to straighten up an expression she didn't realize was showing on the outside of her but was shining like the sun on her face!

We know how the H.G." s experience of romantic love shares reward pathways with a range of substance and behavior addictions, it may influence the drug and/or behavior addiction response. "PROOF" states indeed, abstinent smokers has shown that intense romantic love attenuate brain activity associated with cigarette cue-reactivity.

Feelings of romantic love can progress into feelings of calm attachment, and because attachment engages more plastic forebrain regions, where a long time calm is often a positive state experienced by almost all humans; but drugs is classified as a chemical that has a chemical release from the H.G.

Romantic love have not been categorized as chemical or behavior addition. Embracing data on romantic natural "sensory lust" often felt as positive, but also powerfully negative addition, and its neural similarity to many substance and non-substance addictive states.

Heart break-an almost universal human experience that can trigger stalking, clinical depressants, suicide, homicide, and other crimes of passion. What has God got to do with our passions? Who is really in charge of our 5 senses? "PROOF" will answer that question but let me warn you; whom so ever God joins, let no man separate.

Their H.G. will be bathing both the man and his love with all those love hormones that absolutely would bombard and allow universal human experiences that can trigger stalking, clinical depressants, suicide, homicide, and other crimes of the imitation of love. The passion of the lust of our flesh; passion becoming heart aches, headaches, and heartbreaks.

The judge has a lot of ruling to do when it comes to the outcome of this passion that only felt like, but ended up like cocaine and 100 proof alcohol in our veins and now, where is the love that was supposed to last a life time? If you made a baby out of that passion that now is over; you can be sure that the two of you were never "joined by God," but through dancing skin to skin, you become one flesh **in** the conception as long as that child lives!

"PROOF" will tell you the truth in the difference between what God permit you to do and what God never gave anyone the power to do. Everyone can **control** themselves by saying no or **choose** who they lust over and who they join their sexual organs with and who and how many times they do this and how many people they become parents together (one flesh) with. (rape and incest excluded)

We all can count how many children we have, now if they are all by one person, then you have become one flesh with just that one person; but if you have become parents with different sexual partners, then you have become one flesh with each of them which has nothing to do with love, marriage or even God! "PROOF" will tell you that the very beginning of God joining a man with one woman for as long as they both shall breathe is the only bone that keeps them "together."

The both of them will never share any deoxyribonucleic acid together no matter if they never **dance** together in intimacy, or if they never have a conception together with their bodies making new life, or on the other hand no matter how many children they conceive together. They are sealed in the spirit of love that will never change!

There is a total misunderstanding about **when** two people **become** married, and yet become one flesh; true marriage is not given to us by a law or a right or even a choice. The joining of one man with one woman involuntarily; which cannot be altered by anything they may have agreed to with anyone else even by law!

"PROOF" will remind you that there is nothing stronger than love; not death, or any force, and even the bible reassures us all that against love, there is no law! it's a spirit that God gives to whom He wills without you interfering. Whether you have waited for God to give you His gift in love is another book for me to write!

Oh God forgive us our trespasses against you! Glass houses are fragile; like lust building a house on the sand, when the winds and storms of life beat vehemently upon that weak foundation, it cannot stand and like our glass houses (5 senses) and (emotional) lust relationships are soon faded and gone like tumble weeds blowing as pollution in the wind.

I have read that there were men in the bible that had become **one flesh** with **many** women. Eve had Seth, Abel, Luluwa, Awan, but Cain was of his father the Devil; "PROOF" that two different flesh, one was with Adam and the other was Lucifer, the spirit that was cast down and was called the deceiver of man!

"PROOF" has one question for you to ponder; why do you think the serpent was more subtle than anything else made in the garden?

This was the characteristic of a female, but that is another deception that the eyes still play on males today.

I have not forgotten about the "dancing between Man and Wo," believe me, they are about to get with it, and keep this dance going because the H.G. is not stopping!

"PROOF" is stating that there is a deception in us all that we should not be led by our sensory organs except for the things that are occupied by space; love, intimacy of love and conception are exclusive rights of the spirit of God, and only God controls the amount and the longevity of your H.G. in love of life and to the end of life!

"PROOF" undeniably; L.B.A.C. Love begins not at the conscientiousness which is the way we see God in our own way; but in the "spiritual whelm of God." It is not where you go to find truth; truth is not lost. It is understanding what life is and understanding that love is without the condition, and depredations of lust that only come and go with the vanities of our fleshly desires! Here today and gone tomorrow. Now you see it, and now you don't!

It is here that you should be reminded that we are not supposed to swear; in anything in Heaven or in earth, but we are to let God swear by **His** spirit that we will do this or that. God has put Mann and Wo together with the love that only God can give; the two will have their H.G. sending those love hormones going through their bodies even should they live to be centenarians making that dance together!

Wo is one rare woman; it has been a challenge to just say no to drugs, and let's not forget the use of birth control pills, patches, sprays, foam etc., but the rewards have paid off in her life in many forms and one is having "self-control."

Just use self-control! "PROOF" is not going into details of the reasons drugs are bad for your health; we all know and understand this to be true, but "PROOF" will take this a step farther and tell you that drugs will hinder your H.G. from ever producing the true love connection that draws a female in a bond of trust and devotion that one man must share with one woman.

"PROOF" must stress the misfortune of having an addiction upon drugs whether it be cigarettes, alcohol or other drugs; love cannot be second in your life. **"Love only loves whom is in-love with love!" Lust comes and goes with the flow; if you have the feeling, then most don't fight it. Just realize that the cheap thrills of hormones don't stay long; sometimes leaving behind more than memories, such as the heartaches of sickness, diseases and even criminal acts of that may never be overlooked and forgotten by society.**

Mann and Wo have no addictions, but then again, love is a true addiction if it is to last a lifetime between one man and one woman. The H.G. is dedicated to giving a lifetime of dopamine, serotonin, endorphin and oxytocin making good feelings and smiles until the last breath do them part do them part!

Being Inlove is one addiction that is a natural high and Mann and Wo do not want a cure; there is no cure from love, you got to live with it. "PROOF" proves that no body rips out their healthy heart; and nobody that has life-love wants to give this love back; not even Romeo and Juliet. They rather die than live without it.

Wo's hormones have not been tampered with; she is not in her twenty's any longer, but she still has her menses on a 28 days cycle; 3 days to clean out her Nest" and she is also one of the females that could feel her egg release from her fallopian tube about the 15th of every month just like clockwork. This feeling is called mittelschmerz pain; just a little twitching of light pain that is not hardly more than a wrinkle of the nose effect and it's gone until next month.

"PROOF" stands for truth even when truth is denied; as it has been for years, even as people turn their faces and refuse to admit that O.L.B.A.C. Nevertheless, life energy goes on as the sperm cells of Wo and Mann are given censored hormonal energy from each of their prospective hormones.

Early that very morning Wo felt the egg released from her ovary. In this month's cycle her right fallopian tube twitched with the electron's energy. Her central nervous system messaging in her brain, as she registered tingles and cramping; but she hardly gave it more than a passing thought. Wo's egg has 24 hours of life energy to wait for the sperm and be fertilized.

"PROOF" knows that the ovary of the right-side yields ova which on fertilization develops as males, and the ovary on her left side yields ova which are potentially female! From now on, you will not have to guess whether it will be boy or a girl; just check the side you feel your egg release from! Of course, dopamine has the credit and honor due from **sparking the energy** and cellular motion for the release of that golden egg!

"PROOF" will stop dragging things on with the homeostasis of both Mann and Wo as "dancing" will get heated and stirred up. Cajoling hormones inside the cavity of the organ H.G. which is the gland that secrets hormones currently is raising the roof between Mann and Wo.

Wo does know this joy she feels when she hears Mann's voice is more than she ever imagined! Wo has a smile that is beginning to be questioned by her family as she has been asked several times lately "what have you been up to lately Wo, with that chest cat smile all over your face?" "Oh!" she replied; trying to straighten up an expression she didn't realize was showing on the outside of her but was shining like the sun on her face!

We know how the H.G." s experience of romantic love shares reward pathways with a range of substance and behavior addictions, it may influence the drug and/or behavior addiction response. "PROOF" states indeed, abstinent smokers has shown that intense romantic love attenuate brain activity associated with cigarette cue-reactivity.

Feelings of romantic love can progress into feelings of calm attachment, and because attachment engages more plastic forebrain regions, where a long time calm is often a positive state experienced by almost all humans; but drugs is classified as a chemical that has a chemical release from the H.G.

Romantic love have not been categorized as chemical or behavior addition. Embracing data on romantic natural "sensory lust" often felt as positive, but also powerfully negative addition, and its neural similarity to many substance and non-substance addictive states.

Heart break-an almost universal human experience that can trigger stalking, clinical depressants, suicide, homicide, and other crimes of passion. What has God got to do with our passions? Who is really in charge of our 5 senses?

"PROOF" will answer those questions, but let me warn you, whom so ever God joins, let no man's heart be broken; because their H.G. will be bathing both the man and his love with all those love hormones. Absolutely will not allow universal human experience that can trigger stalking, clinical depressants, suicide, homicide, and other crimes of the imitation of love called the passion of the lust of our flesh; passion's heart aches, headaches, and heartbreaks!

The judge has a lot of ruling to do when it comes to the outcome of this passion that only felt like, but ended up like cocaine and 100 proof alcohol in our veins and now, where is the love that was supposed to last a life time? If you made a baby out of that passion that now is over; you can be sure that the two of you were never "joined by God," but through dancing skin to skin, you became one flesh **in** the conception!

"PROOF" will tell you the truth in the difference between what God permit you to do and what God never gave anyone the power to do. Everyone can **control** themselves by saying no or **choose** who they lust over and who they join their sexual organs with and who and how many times they do this and how many people they become parents together (one flesh) with. (rape and incest excluded)

We all can count how many children we have, now if they are all by one person, then you have become one flesh with just that one person; but if you have become parents with different sexual partners, then you have become one flesh with each of them which has nothing to do with love, marriage or even God! "PROOF" will tell you that the very beginning of God joining a man with one woman for as long as they both shall breathe is the only bone that keeps them "together."

The both of them will never share any deoxyribonucleic acid together no matter if they never **dance** together in intimacy, or if they never have a conception together with their bodies making new life, or on the other hand no matter how many children they conceive together. They are sealed in the spirit of love that will never change!

There is a total misunderstanding about **when** two people **become** married, and yet become one flesh; true marriage is not given to us by a law or a right or even a choice. The joining of one man with one woman involuntarily; which cannot be altered by anything they may have agreed to with anyone else even by law!

"PROOF" will remind you that there is nothing stronger than love; not death, or any force, and even the bible reassures us all that against love, there is no law! it's a spirit that God gives to whom He wills without you interfering.

Whether you have waited for God to give you His gift in love is another book for me to write! Oh God forgive us our trespasses against you! Glass houses are fragile; like lust building a house on the sand, when the winds and storms of life beat vehemently upon that weak foundation, it cannot stand and like our glass houses (5 senses) and (emotional) lust relationships are soon faded and gone like tumble weeds blowing as pollution in the wind.

I have read that there were men in the bible that had become **one flesh** with **many** women. Eve had Seth, Abel, Luluwa, Awan, but Cain was of his father the Devil; "PROOF" that two different flesh, one was with Adam and the other was Lucifer, the spirit that was cast down and was called the deceiver of man!

"PROOF" has one question for you to ponder; why do you think the serpent was more subtle than anything else made in the garden? This was the characteristic of a female, but that is another deception that the eyes still play on man today.

Before Mann and Wo began to get busy dancing and tingling skin to skin; let's go to a time where "PROOF" and the "tree of knowledge" and the medical books agree that there is a forbidden fruit that is in a guarded area that is in the mist or center of the garden in which God protects! It's not an apple; even though it is the fruit of the loom, and it is to be private.

God has spiritually led us to know, but we just don't understand to obey this knowledge. So, God has put a lock down on our private garden and the fruit it bears with a warning to all that trespass against it. Even though we read that Adam (Cain) and Eve and everybody else along with Abraham (Ishmael) and Sari who choose to use their own plans to this private garden and got fruit of undesirable results.

"PROOF" once again has all the answers to not only tell you where the garden is but will let you go right to your own guarded garden; a garden that is "Private." This private place is to be off limits except to the time when God joins us together with our other half.

The sons of God; never seem to stop lusting after us; just like back in the day when Humans saw the daughters of man that they were beautiful to look upon and God's spirit was kindled, reports the K.J.V. The courts of "fruit" support is updated daily with documentational evidence.

Runaway-wild-weed-passion-of-lust never was a flower of love, now is mowed down into missing action of the H.G. simply not sending out those oxytocin, serotonin, and endorphin of happy bliss sometime after conception; causing millions of men to be trapped and snared by their identity left behind in the female private garden, that became prison passion gates.

Ask any man to tell you what is the price for "freedom" from the grips of the private garden when you trespass against it? Their sperm inside the doors of the ovum cajoled by the hormone secreted by H.G. called dopamine; convicts him. The paternity courts by this "PROOF" of evidence. The identity bonded and sealed as one flesh of deoxyribonucleic acid forever trapped devouring the forbidden fruit of the private garden!

"PROOF" will spell out the lust that we called love, but it never was love at all; it was a deception of the kind that has been known to man long before Eve was created in the garden of Eden. (Gen. 2:15) The viewing of the garden was just another plot of evil for Adam to be tempted.

Adam lusted after what he saw going on around him; but he was told (Gen. 2:16) Adam was shown everything and told, freely eat; then (Gen. 2:17) he could look, but don't touch the fruit. Adam was tempted as a single minded male then and there! "That Woman" who was the fruit of passion with no love intended, deceived Adam! (Gen. 2:17) The warning was given to Adam after the seed of temptation was planted; Adam's eyes were opened then, he saw what the animals were doing, he was no dummy! (Gen. 2:18) What Adam was doing in the garden, was not good; he found nothing "fit "him!

"That Woman," was not his mate, she did not belong to him. Who was she? She was not Eve. "PROOF" proves (Gen.2:20) between The God of this world and Adam everything had a name; Eve was named by Adam, but "That Woman!" was forever nameless until the man is caught with fear from being with her. "That Woman" is her name today that the man know the Devil gives to men today that is not of God. God only gives a man his mate, and he knows her name! My name is "Norah!" My husband knows my name!

"PROOF" proves that women have been noted for changing their minds; affecting up to 80% of women. Affected by our cycles every day of the month. Hormone levels constantly changing in her brain and body, even being more biological and mystical perceived as intuition.

"That woman that you gave to me; she gave it to me and I did eat," but note that in the court of law, you have the right to be silent, and if you give up that right, anything can, and will be used against you? Eve! She has been guilted all through the picture; even to this very day.

Wasn't Adam the one she called "Lord" an endearing title given to a woman's husband and notice Eve never said anything to be recorded over Cain murdering her Son Able or of him being put out of the garden! Eve rejoiced at the birth of Seth saying "I have gotten another good seed from the lord; she referred to Adam as Lord.

Eve only had 2 good seeds, Able and Seth. Cain was **not** her "good" son! Lord Adam was Eve's husband, father of Abel and Seth; but Cain's father was of the Devil being Lucifer, the god of this world, the serpent.

K.J.V. read Cain was of his father the Devil. The power of suggestion that Adam was the Devil, but you know again there was another one missing, being the Devil. Throwing rocks and hiding his hands,

How could the womb of Eve conceive that which came from the devil? What was Adam and Eve's blood type? "PROOF" will tell you this much, Cain was the son of the Devil that transformed himself into a form that seduced Adam. Lucifer knew there was nothing "fit" for him, in Genesis 2:16, before Eve was made in Genesis 2:20.

"PROOF" recalls how the woman was caught in the very act of adultery in the K.J.V. another bad scene where the man tried to lay all the guilt on the woman; but Jesus knew that the only way to catch the woman in the very act of adultery was while the man was still having sex with her! DUH!

"PROOF" proves if this was a case in a court of law, Eve would not be found guilty because Adam did not know the name of the female he slept with! He just said, "that woman." Who to this day have seen "that woman" that slept with Adam? Tell that story to a Judge? You don't have enough supporting evidence for a substantial case.

The bible was written by men inspired by God; we are inspired by God as well to understand there were some omitted, things not recorded, and the name of "that woman" was not recorded, but "PROOF" will prove to you Adam did not say "Eve," that wife, that mate that you gave to me; it was just "that woman."

Power of suggestion, over there in the mist of the garden, "***that*** woman!" Adam knew the difference between Eve and "that woman." I can bet you can see him pointing to the thickets saying, "That Woman. That you gave"

God gave Adam a mate that was blessed and fit for him; and their children together were of a blessed seed, because they were of the same blood-type. Eve was not made for the serpent and even today blood-type of the O type blood female such as Eve would be compatible completely with Adam. However, the case may be; Adam knew why there was nothing that fit him in the animal yard, because "that woman" that the god of this world gave him, being that serpent beguiled him!

Even the doctors will tell us all today that which the bible has said all along; the life of the body Is in the blood and everyone in the world still being deceived to believe the serpent danced with Eve; but noticed the Serpent was the beguiled woman that had been transformed into being.

The mastermind deceiver and the author of confusion. "That Woman" was not given a name; you just assumed it was Eve, but Lucifer transformed himself as an Angel of light; the first strange woman that was made! Lucifer was his own worst enemy. "PROOF" asks you this question; You knew Satan was cast down; God made him the "god of this world", and he is the deceiver. The question is are you part of the world that is still blinded by his deceptions? Satan would deceive the very elect of God if it were possible; but it is not possible to deceive the elect of God. K.J.V.

Adam is no different than any other male today; how many males have been deceived by what he sees. Beauty, and sexy; allowing himself to be enticed and seduced by the crafty spirit of Lucifer and then blame "that woman" that is missing.

"PROOF" proves the point of deception that it is not always what you say; but what you didn't say. What is done in the dark will be brought to light; Adam pointed not at Eve, but that woman (over there) that he didn't know that had no name that was given to him for just one thing by the god of the garden. The woman that was not good and fit for him of lust; she was both the "spiritual" mother and father of Cain.

Adam was commanded not to touch the fruit in the garden while Eve was still unmade! Often like most women today, takes the blame, but Eve did not have to speak up for her Innocence, she was saved in childbirth and that is by not giving birth to a demon seed!

"That-woman;" was not only the Serpent; but the strange woman that was not "fit" for Adam. She was "that woman" given to him by, for and of Lucifer; and then Adam asked for a mate out of loneness; his mate had a name; she shall be called Eve! More than a woman, Eve was a companion of his own, right, skin, blood-type blessed by God. "PROOF" proves with evidence of medical, biological and Biblical knowledge that agree that many court rulings were solved by the blood matching. There are discriminations that we were born with; what blood type are you? Our deoxyribonucleic acid is our life blood.

There is many secrets as there are mysteries in the tree of good and evil; but "PROOF" proves that O.L.B.A.C. being the most secret ever held. Between the veil of what not only is said, but what is not said, and what has been completely omitted; there is a world going on unknown! The power of suggestion and the element of surprise is the very basis our 5 senses are founded upon, this is the religion that is the hope born from the conception of deception!

Human logic and the evidence of playing and gambling one state of senses enticing them, testing and leaving them on their own feelings. We all finally succumbed, acting from the sense of selfishness, greediness and demanding ones on way to be given out of pride and worldly gain.

Our 5 senses lead to the err of our blindness and the blind cant lead the blind, for they both fall into the ditch. Humans use their common sense to help find their way in a world of forms, yet "Soul love" the spirit that joins an inner part of a man to one woman for life of love and peace only comes from God.

"PROOF" proves that life is energy that creates; our life, and the love of our lives. In our own eyes we can only see what is on the outside of a person; and that person can only see what we allow to dare to show and tell them, but God is the spirit that is not limited by conditions and things that hinder the peace that only is of God and given to us by God through Love, Love like Mann and Wo!

Let me just invite you to sip with me on your favorite juice, or coffee even though it's too late for coffee. I need to ease into a mood to cajole your H.G. as I turn our minds to the Song of Solomon which is a beautiful love story, until I read and studied these scriptures; only then did I realize that even though Solomon had lots of wives around him; they all were begging king Solomon to "dance with them!"

"PROOF" taking you out to the field; let us get up early to the vineyards. Let us see if the vine flourish, whether the tender grape appear, and the pomegranates bud forth; there will I give thee my love. The mandrakes give a smell, and at our gates are all manner of pleasant fruits, new and old, which I have for thee, o my beloved. Remember Adam was in the garden with Lucy!

"Solomon had a vineyard at Baal Hamon; he let out the vineyard unto the keepers; everyone for the fruit thereof was to bring a thousand pieces of silver." "My vineyard, which is mine, is before me: thou, O Solomon, must have a thousand, and those that keep the fruit thereof-two hundred." "Thou that dewellest in the gardens, the companions hearken to thy voice: cause me to hear it." "PROOF" reminds you to know that the god of this world really lay the temptation on thick as honey when Adam was shown the garden!

"Make hast, my beloved, and be thou like a roe or to a young hart upon the mountains of spices." "PROOF" went through the bible to the most loved scriptures K.J.V. where you have been given "PROOF" that King Solomon was said to have great wisdom, but he also had great folly to which he admits to this.

His folly which means foolishness in **earthly** wisdom was in many pleasures. One of his foolish follies were his acquired harem. Adam has great wisdom, but he has a weakness for being lonely. Then after he found pleasure with "that Woman," then he realized she was not fit for him.

Of course, God only gives a man one wife. Adam and his fall from grace, Noah in the great flood, Abraham denied his wife publicly calling her "his sister," Job bemoans God in dust sack cloth and ashes just to name a few Godly Men, to the "PROOF: that God has men that he gave wives to and they loved that one and only wife unto death.

The word harem could mean cup bearer, but it is more likely to mean mistress, lover or concubine. It could also be quite a crude term which refers to women solely as sexual objects. How very 21st century. There is after all nothing new under the sun. King Solomon lusted with many women besides Pharaohs daughter.

All in all, Solomon had seven hundred wives of royal births and three hundred concubines, and his lawful-paper-wives lead him astray! Lust through sex would not satisfy. If sex would satisfy then you would expect that Solomon would have been satisfied, but of all the women Solomon and anyone can meet; if a man gain the whole world and lose or never meet his soulmate, he has profited nothing as in the eyes of God! He must be given favor through a God given Wife.

"PROOF" understands it takes time to make changes in our lives; but changes happens slowly and as time goes on things seem to just happen. That's the way it is inside the H.G. of Mann also! Mann is "100% male" let him tell us in his own words. Go figure! Color has nothing to do with love whether it's the color of skin or your favorite hue; love is color blind to the physical senses of the connections we call beauty.

Beauty is only skin deep; but "PROOF" digs deep into the body seeing a beauty of the hormones that make beauty take on a new form; beauty in the form of a woman. Woman is man's glory; glory is another word for "beauty," The covering over the head of a woman is her husband; let not her head be uncovered!

Woman was given to Adam as a gift of favor; beauty that surrounds the true gift of God. This rare beauty is Wo; she is the Soulmate that Mann is so joyful over! Mann is a very busy one; up early and hardly taking time to slow down before the day shadows end in the night moon under his sleeping eyelids. Dreams of wonder fill his heart of the voice that came with sunshine and joy! God did not let us choose him or each other in marriage; God chooses us!

Mann had to be sensible about this thing! After all, he has his understanding that he has never in his life felt like this; he shook his head in amazement for some time now and it is something that just won't be moved! Many waters cannot quench love, neither can the floods drown it: if a man would give all his substances of his house for love, it would utterly be contemned. Many waters cannot quench love, neither can the floods drown it: if a man would give all his substances of his house for love, it would utterly be contemned.

The very thought of that voice made his heart smile, and he knew it was love! Oh, Mann wrestled and reasoned with himself repeatedly, but still he knew he had never been happier over anything like this woman has made him. What did he know about her? Nothing but her name. The very split second he heard her voice, the H.G. secreted by the release on the thousand actively neutrons charged with electrical activity. Oxytocin released into the blood stream when these cells are excited.

What is so remarkable, this hormone just electrically gave Mann a involuntarily shot of "trust" for Wo! Oxytocin comes into sharper focus; its social radius of action turns out to have definite limits. The love and trust it promotes are not toward the world in general, just toward a person" in-group. Oxytocin turns out to be the hormone of the clan, north universal brotherhood. "PROOF" now concludes that oxytocin is the agent of ethnocentrism.

What is ethnocentrism? The evaluation of other cultures according to preconceptions originating in the standards and customs of one own culture. Before you go off on a whim; "PROOF" has all the answers here, just keep reading! Remember we are being wise not leaning to our own understanding, but to the wisdom of medical, biblical and God!

We are not to forget that our body is controlled by the H.G. and when it sends out the oxytocin into Mann's bloodstream and into his central nervous system with the involuntary motivation to "trust" the voice that his hormone signaled as a "in-group."

Oxytocin did all the guess work for Mann; of course, his body was charged with electrons buzzing him with trust for Wo; they matched! Race, drug usage, faith, blood type, even down to how they were raised, but at this moment, neither of them knew just how perfectly they were matched together.

What does it mean that a chemical basic for such a bonding is embedded in the brain? It is a part of our ancestral environment and very important for us to detect in others whether they had a long-term commitment, it is not something that can be changed by education. There are some negative aspect to oxytocin; the brain weights emotional attitudes like those prompted by oxytocin against information available to the conscious mind.

If there is no cognitive information in a situation in which a decision has to be made, whether to trust a stranger about whom nothing is known, the brain will go with the emotional advice from its's oxytocin system, but otherwise rational data will be weighed against the influence from oxytocin and may well override it.

It's surprising and amazing that a substance like oxytocin can affect such a high-level human behavior; this neurotransmitter can so specifically affect these social behaviors! Mann's oxytocin accepted the voice of Wo after it was analogized and coded to be trustworthy!

"PROOF" can tell you bits and pieces of document evidence of how the brain uses chemically boosters to stimulate the central nervous system of whoever uses their 5 senses on; but Mann is the man that can attest "PROOF" is on point when it comes to what the will of God will do along with his H.G. and Wo! Despite what you have been told; the genders are largely the same neurologically; unless we let Mann tell you, and in his own words "Oh man, I felt joy!"

What Mann felt was positive electro charges of energy exciting his central nervous system; dopamine controlling the excitable movements of the cellular activity that gave Mann such a happy feeling that was aiming his thoughts and affection completely on the very **Soul** belonging to a voice so endearing from a woman named Wo!

Beauty in in the eye of the beholder; in this case, Mann saw a spiritual glory that only his spirit could see, and he was bombastic overjoyed! Lust of the eyes or the lust of his flesh had nothing to do with how Mann felt; he had never laid eyes on Wo, he felt this was the very instant he heard her say "hello" then "lights" went on and he knew warmth of love for Wo!

"PROOF" will tell you that in there are many ways that men can find pleasing in human traits. Lust of pleasure happens voluntarily, any time, or stop any time. People can know each other for years before one day the "hook" catches, or lets you go! This was not what happens when "love" happens. Love is involuntary; love draws the forces between two people destined to be together by spiritual rights.

Most people in the world have a drive to reproduce. This can lead to negative and positive behaviors, on the negative side, some men may feel the need to be womanizers. They may seek out and sleep with several women at the same time. Many cultures glorify this behavior; but the difference between love and lust are these factors.

Love is involuntary, lust is voluntary. Love is between a man and one woman only for the remainder of their lives whether they ever become one flesh with a child. Lust is temporal and is shared with whoever, whenever, however, and anything like that which goes along with our basic voluntary short-lived actions as messages to the H.G. that secretes hormones.

"PROOF" has no nerve, just keeps the balls rolling when it states that Love is a spiritual state; lust is just a mental state. There was more than what Mann could ever imagine going on inside his heart as one day he knew that he and Wo were more to each other than mere words could express; more than anything physical could ever do. The two decided to meet!

When two people first meet face to face for the very first time; when they have a force much greater than themselves working in them both which is the will of God; great things have been planned for them that is beyond their wildest dreams! O.L.B.A.C. and this new life began at conception also!

They both had the love of God working in their lives before they ever met; now with that very love that God loved them individualistically, now there was no separation of that love between them. They both felt the same love of God for each other from the very first "Hello." This is the "joining" that only God hath "joined."

This involuntarily will of God. I charge you, O daughters of Jerusalem, that ye stir not up, nor awake my love, until he please. Who is this that cometh up from the wilderness, leaning upon her beloved?

I raised thee up under the apple tree: there thy mother brought: there she brought thee forth that bare thee, "Set me as a seal upon thine heart, as a seal upon thine arm: for love is as strong as death; jealousy is cruel as the grave: the coals thereof are the coals of fire, which hath a most vehement flame."

Oxytocin raced upon the portal of the neuron's energy within him as his quiet firm footsteps drew him into the portal where the magnetic connection of "life-spirit-love," and their "soul" embracing his joy, his God chosen gift of favor! When a man findeth a wife, (God does not give girlfriends) he findeth a good thing and obtained favor from the Lord! What is this favor?

Mann's heart was beating out love to Wo as he beheld her for the very first time, his wife given by God! Wo was so cajoled by his presence allowing their form to align skin to skin, one soul joined spiritually together in-love! Here is the "PROOF" that love begins at conception; the very moment they meet! L.B.A.C. the moment it is conceived! "I am a wall and my breast like towers then was I in his eyes as one that found favor."

H.G. is the very most important organ the we cannot live, conceive or love without! "PROOF" is so bold to say; you can't even try to live without it; conception can't begin without it, and that involuntary "love-spark" of the hormones giving that good feeling that lasts till the last breath only comes from the H.G. under the control of God!

Wo has found favor in the eyes of Mann; he has set her as a seal upon his heart, H.G. has sparked every pumping of his heart with love energy! The H.G. which controls all the hormones in the body, responds to their arousal. It signals the body to produce testosterone. It's hard for men to feel an orgasm if they have a low level of this hormone. Vasopressin is the hormone responsible for aggression, memories, and concentration in both sexes.

It also constricts blood vessels. Its secretion affects men's arousal. However, in women the increase of Vasopressin caused by anger or stress reduces sexual desire. In women the luteinizing hormone is positively correlated with sexual excitement the female has only one entrance in her body where the male's body is designed to enter that will lead to conception. It is more than his pleasure to be cajoled by dopamine as he points his aim, bowing in that direction!

This excitement makes Bartholin glands produce further lubrication; of course, we must add that the H.G. is Mann's Homologous to bulbourethral glands located in the deep perineal pouch where mucus is secreted as "fuel-oil" to lubricate Wo's vagina;

gliding and knocking his way through heaven! Activity in different parts of the brain also increases.

One of these parts is the amygdala. It participates in processing memory, decision making, and emotional responses, but the activity of the part of the brain responsible for memories decreases. Maybe this is because Mann and Wo don't care about memory recall and other associated emotions during their dance

Mann & Wo become suspended within themselves weightless flying to the moon; with the sparks between them; believe "PROOF'S" witnessing to the powerful effects of love between a man and his God given wife. Since God has joined the both together spiritually; they know that they don't have to swear to each other that they will stay together until the last breath. The Bible states that man should not swear before Heaven or by anything that is in earth; God is to preform your oaths and carry them out, because nothing will separate.

"PROOF" proves the law just ask a you to pay for a license and asked by the judge or Minister "do you TAKE" each other? They are never asked if God has joined them, so in this case; the judge just assumes that God has given them to each other in love! Nothing shall separate the ones that God joins in love!

God does not change through time or chance. People change; but God change not, and God is not a man that He should lie, or the son of man that He should repent! Who really repented over making Man in the garden? God does not change, or repent, or make mistakes; neither does God bow, but in the garden, the world is deceived along with Adam over who was who. "PROOF" must tell the truth the truth without bias! Solomon had wisdom to everything other than the one thing that God withheld; "LOVE!" All King Solomon knew was "LUST of his eyes, flesh, and the pride of life.

All is vanity saith the preacher man! Solomon said there is nothing new under the sun; but Mann and Wo have a "New Day under the sun." What does it feel like to know what you have is love and not lust? Mann and Wo know from the very beginning that this was something different. They learned as time went on that they both shared the same feeling; and they both knew that God had everything to do it.

The surreal feeling of it all was; this love was a gift that they both treasured from God. A gift that they had a spiritual right to love one another and to be one with each other-half of a single body! Holding each other in this love was being in Heaven together; in a sense, they were! The night must come; the night is the time for love, the time for a special "dance" between the bodies that is joined by God in love!

I am my beloved's, and his desire is towards me. (why is King Solomon writings comparing the addiction of drugs and intoxication, to that the addiction for his beloved?) I will go up to the palm tree, I will take hold of his boroughs thereof, now also thy breast shall be of clusters of the vine, and the smell of thy nose lie apples. The roof of thy mouth like the best wine for my beloved, that goeth down sweetly, causing the lips of those that are asleep to speak. I am my beloved's, and his desire is towards me.

The kisses that Mann gave Wo was the kind that would suggest he had kissed her before. Tender, patiently he stroked Wo's lips; loving touches, yet passionately suggestive. Tiny embers of fire danced between them as they tasted the skin of their very Soul!

Their breath vaporized between their lips as one breath; fueling the rapture taking them both up into a place where neither had shared with anyone before, and no one shall love like them, after them. Ever!

Inside the very brains of the two captured hearts beating as one Soul; the sparks of oxytocin, dopamine, serotonin endorphin are influencing a dance between Mann and Wo that will cause a bond with their brains sealed in memory.

A memory that they both will cherish between them always; this will be the communion of celebrating giving themselves to each other in a physical form. Knowing that God gave them to each other; being together makes them both enjoy the freedom and peace, that flows of warmth, from the kindled glow within them.

As the world turned and there was no more searching for love in all the wrong faces and places lay the bodies of one Soul encircled together in a dance made for Angels! "PROOF" now goes pass where demons dare not to tread; getting only as close as the sighs of passions turn into sleep.

Blessed with the real thing called love, Mann and Wo's dance continues as the music is silently played within them; the harmony of the hormones pick up the melody between the pages of the sheet where life-love is consummated.

Mann could not help to bow lower before the other half of his Soul. A delight that lifted them into a joy that only the two of them would know. Hormones keeping the charges going; every one of these hormones knew their way to "San Jose!"

The only ones that were feeling giddy were Mann and Wo; they were so close, closer than they not only been with each other, but the heaven they were going to were only traveled by them alone. The narrow road inside Wo's vagina was inviting for Mann; estrogen and progesterone spread out like a carpet of silk and soft satin, as he plunged deeper into Wo's warmth drowning within the sweetest of pleasure, again!

kisses exchanged a thousand times as to where Wo's nose and lips began to blush like roses kissed by the sun. the bodies that were separate became one for as long as the dance continued; as one night and all through the wee hours of the morning, they danced in the silent music of Soulove! Linked her together by skin to his skin within; Touching, kissing, as the dance goes on, the peripheral nervous system gets a signal and forwards it to both of their H.G deeper within each of them.

Finally, the true meaning of love from God is understood; **"Wo-Man,"** God has put the two halves together! They share the same blood-type, the same background, compatibility in their D.N.A. the background history were compatible to one another.

Their bodies blended into the other one as the sparking entwined their very skin; two halves, positive and negative sides. A right and the left! Many songs that come to mind right now seem to fit the tune that dance in rhythm within their hearts. Mann is feeling so passionate, yet he could only contain this passion at bay for so long; he just knew Wo was the other half of his self! King Solomon spoke of grapes, and palm trees and what may have him in the garden; but Mann was feasting on milk and honey that only love can supply.

Whether you **dance** in lust or love; bodies have *feeling of emotions. If your dance is of lust; this may be your only dance together which may end up making you forever **one flesh together in a conception of a baby** with someone you will never be "joined in love!" To be joined together is a "Spiritual gift;" to be blessed, chosen to be **in-love** together whereas no law or force shall be able to separate.*

*The dance of the physical bodies is a special gift the chosen present to each other as gifts; a treasure no one has received before! No one can duplicate them. The word chosen means "Anointed," in the case of God giving one woman to one man having been selected as the best or most appropriate. When the couple come to be intimate; they give their bodies to each other as the offering of themselves to their other half. This offering or gift of intimacy "PROOF" honors as **"The dance of love."***

This dance will not make them share the same blood type, or the same D.N.A., or be anything more or less than what they were before the dance. If a couple were not joined by God; dancing all night will not persuade God to give you his blessing in a marriage of faith. When you have been joined by God's spirit; if one never dances together in this unity, they still will be one in the spirit of marriage.

God joints spiritually; man and woman gives their bodies as a token of their love to each other, and the conception of a child is a blessing God presents to the couple as the longevity of their genes being one flesh together.

"PROOF" proves that sex or marriage within itself does not cause any couple to end up with the same D.N.A. However, to make this point very clear; you can get up from dancing and find you both are now joined with an S.T.D., Indeed, you have become one bad thing together! Sadly, maybe later discover a conception that will have joined D.N.A. from the both of you; with maybe S.T.D.

Deep within the hypothalamus gland secreting out passion, trust and rapture bliss as a chemical that is inspiring, but complex of a feeling too hard to explain with science. What the chemical processes in our brains can clarify what we feel in moments of intimacy. Desire may come spontaneously or be encouraged by stimulation.

looking at pictures activate the brain H.G. and the feeling of desire. Spontaneous desire usually appears when you're falling in love with a partner. In a lustful relationship, however, the drive usually comes after erotic stimulation or by the feeling of emotional or physical intimacy.

We can choose our partners with social, cultural, economic and even by genetic factors in mind basic by our voluntary actions. God chooses who we are to love by a will that is involuntary action on part of H.G.

Mann and Wo had a spontaneous desire that sparked without ever touching or even seeing the other one; their Love was not built from stimulation or physical intimacy. Excitement and desire are very hard to distinguish, but "PROOF" can separate them.

Usually scientists define excitement as the physiological body response to something such as changes in genitalia. It is also important to know that excitement can still occur even if a person doesn't feel any sexual desire.

This wedding bed was not defiled; meaning what God had joined, was good, and no man had defiled her! "PROOF" will be the first to agree with you that thinking about S.T.D., birth control, or any other negativity at this time would stop any one from dancing; Mann and Wo have been chosen by God for this moment of gift giving; God gave them skin to feel and they are drug free, disease free and this is their O. M. G. dance!

Mann and Wo are sparking in the star lit- electron lights of their passion. The neurotransmitter dopamine is to be thanked for the response to sexual stimulation. Mann and Wo really do feel explosive excitement. In addition, arousal causes an output of nitrogen oxide and noradrenaline. These substances increase blood to their genitalia to initiate an erection, lubrication, and the enlargement of labia.

This sparking is a spark that spark not only from skin to skin; but deep within their bodies, as the H.G. Steadily secreted endorphin, oxytocin, serotonin throughout the central nervous systems of Mann and Wo. H.G. The motherboard of Wo (H.G.) takes control; if any time females take charge, is within her own body. "PROOF" will prove that female cajoles and controls all 500 million sperm once inside her body with the very powerful hormone of dopamine!

Dopamine is just one of 7 chemical hormones; an electrical neurotransmitter that travels through both male and female central nervous system. **Dopamine cajoles** the desire, pleasure, contentment motivation **electrical spark**, and the chemistry in **deoxyribonucleic acid**. In both Man and Wo, dopamine is happy to cajole them; let's start with Wo and her being **cajoled by the spark of life that is dopamine**!

This energy is stored and secreted in her motherboard (H.G.) This **"motherboard is a bad girl"** in Wo, and "PROOF" is so excited to prove! Life begins at conception; always, life is energy that is alive! The H.G. is directly connected to the posterior lobe of Wo's pituitary gland controlling by **regulating** the both parts of her pituitary gland by sending signals to **release** or **inhibit** pituitary **hormone** production by means of neurons.

This is an **involuntary** action! Wo's pituitary gland is in perfect health; if it doesn't produce enough follicle-stimulating hormone or luteinizing hormones, it might cause problems with sexual functions, menstruation and fertility, short height, infertility, tolerance to cold, fatigue, and inability to produce breast milk!

Vaginal dryness, and loss of some female sexual characteristic that "PROOF" will prove to your H.G. is unhealthy and unhappy. In men deficiencies of these hormones results in wasting away (atrophy) of the testes, decreased sperm production and consequent infertility, erectile dysfunction, and loss of some male sexual characteristics.

"PROOF: proves that poor tumors that affect the H.G. may cause deficiencies of pituitary hormones. The pituitary may suddenly stop producing hormones, especially ACTH, leading to low levels of blood pressure and glucose in the blood.

There is a battle of the sexes where someone got to win and someone got to lose; no guessing here, "PROOF" has the answer later in this book! Wo has her motherboard supplying her with the right number of hormones cajoling her to be assertive!

Mann is about to dance with a kitten; but her dopamine levels roar from the tigress within her! The femininity, called womanliness or girlishness is a set of attributes, behaviors, and roles generally associated with women and girls. The peak of this hormone occurs before ovulation when a woman's eggs are preparing for fertilization. Some studies even claim that a woman's gait, voice and smell change before ovulation.

Some behaviors considered feminine is socially constructed, some are indicated are biologically influenced. Wo is so very feminine with her soft voice and at the age of over 30 she still has that bouncy pep in her step and sway in her walk that now is being prepared to translate every fiber in her body in a dance of love between her and Mann.

Wo is sweet, gentle overflowing with warmth. Full of modesty and humility yet her affection (**first call**) expressing itself in a tender emotion that cajoles him to her devotion and understanding, Godly wisdom and Old-fashioned characteristics!

Mann's H.G. censored within him the very split second he heard her voice over the phone the very first word that came out of her mouth; "hello!" "PROOF" will state the most important thing that Wo had going for her was "FAITH. Mann was magnetized by the unseen power of energy; that very spark, life-energy that began with their conception of love." Mann's H.G. connected with the sugar and nitrogen acids the very cellular energy that quickened the spiritual involuntary action of "Love" between his "chosen woman."

"Love is involuntary on our part, love has a mind of its own; the H.G. has a major job to do and it does a body good in a heartbeat! partners presence or some action like touching, watching erotic movies or looking at pictures activate the brain H.G. and the feeling of desire. Spontaneous desire usually appears when you're falling in love with a partner.

In a lustful relationship, however, the drive usually comes after erotic stimulation or by the feeling of emotional or physical intimacy. We can choose our partners with social, cultural, economic and even by genetic factors in mind basic by our voluntary actions.

God chooses who we are to love by a will that is involuntary action on part of that within the hypothalamus gland secreting out deep passion, trust and rapture bliss as a chemical that is inspiring, but too complex of a feeling too hard to explain with science, what the chemical processes in our brains can clarify what we feel in moments of intimacy. Desire may come spontaneously or be encouraged by stimulation; only the H.G. determines whether that feeling last till only the **next** or our **last** breath in life together!

The H.G. which controls all the hormones in the body, responds to their arousal. It signals the body to produce testosterone. It's hard for men to feel an orgasm if they have a low level of this hormone. Vasopressin is the hormone responsible for aggression, memories, and concentration in both sexes. It also constricts blood vessels.

This secretion affects men's arousal. However, in women the increase of Vasopressin caused by anger or stress reduces sexual desire. In women the luteinizing hormone is positively correlated with sexual excitement

This excitement makes Bartholin glands produce further lubrication of course we must add that the H.G. is Mann's Homologous to bulbourethral glands located in the deep perineal pouch where mucus is secreted as "fuel-oil" to lubricate Wo's vagina; gliding and knocking his way through heaven! Activity in different parts of the brain also increases.

One of these parts is the amygdala. It participates in processing memory, decision making, and emotional responses, but the activity of the part of the brain responsible for memories decreases. Maybe this is because Mann and Wo don't care about memory recall and other associated emotions during their dance

The highest part of this dance is the period of the plateau phase; sexual excitement prior to orgasm. Heart rate, respiration, pressure, and muscle tension continue to increase throughout. The H.G. constantly busy racing hearts of both lovers; rarely getting above 130 beats per minute, but Mann's blood pressure is pumping blood nearly always staying under 170 (the higher number.)

Wo's blood pressure steady as 120/80; as her clitoris becomes extremely sensitive and withdraws slightly, her panting and gleefulness mounting in Mann's ears, as the perspiration rolled off their bodies in crystal beads turning to pearl.

they intensified their dancing; they felt the heat from their energy, but H.G. did not change their body temperature at 98.6! Wo began to get thirsty, but it was ignored. H.G. was trying to send both stress signals of thirst, hunger pangs; but this was not registered to either of them enough to obey their thirst other than the thirst of love!

H.G. was monitoring the abundances of emotions ready for a hormonal-overdrive; this dance is going to be a marathon! Truly there was a marathon going on, but you must come and go along inside with "PROOF" into the deeper parts of Mann and Wo.

Watch out for the currents; you must be grounded to reduce static electricity, but as you well know, what really matters when it comes to what occupies space is what we are all about, **PROTRONS,**

NEUTRON & ELECTRONS! Beauty is more than skin deep; and there is more to life than what meets the eye.

"PROOF" Declares to you that we should be grateful and thankful that major life decisions are left up to our involuntary actions that are always in God's control monitored within the brain! We control things that can be empty and vain and can be voided out as we change our minds; but the brain is not controlled by our 5 senses alone, but by the unseen power of Permissive and Divine will of life energy through the hypothalamus gland.

"PROOF" proves that MRI scans show that different parts of the brain are involved during orgasm. These parts include the amygdala (memory, and emotions) hypothalamus (subconscious body control) anterior cingulate cortex (impulse control and empathy), and nucleus accumbens (a feeling of euphoria) Overall, there are about 30 active parts of the brain-involved in orgasm.

Sex is a natural painkiller. It triggers the release of endorphin, which reduce pain and stress. Studies show that during vaginal stimulation, sensitivity to discomfort decreases.

Orgasm is the most pleasant and the shortest phase. Women are a bit luckier than men because their orgasms last longer and can experience multiple orgasms, but it's easier for men to get an orgasm. Secretion of the hormone oxytocin leads to rhythmic muscle contraction and ejaculation. The larger the release of oxytocin, the more intense the orgasms accumbens rewards us with a good portion of dopamine that we feel as relaxing pleasure. Active parts of the brain are involved in orgasm.

Muscles relax, the heart rate and breath normalize and the body feels pleasant tiredness; this is the end of the physical dance, Mann has with Wo; skin to skin, but the dance inside the body of the female has just about to begin with her new partner! Interlocking pieces; left with right sides fitting in a dance of cajoling electrical charged neuro transmitted energies; where only the cellular of life energy can light the path to the tunnel of deoxyribonucleic love!

A place where chromosome is not a choice and dividing is involuntary; becoming together in something new from something genetic from what was pasted down from our parents, in this same **involuntary cellular activity** in you and me. This is the spirit of O.L.B.A.C. for us all!

PHASE I

DANCING WITH THE HORMONES WITHIN US!

THE HYPOTHALAMUS GLAND has been doing its job very well; in fact, Mann and Wo gleefully smile with pleasure with no complaints about how they feel dancing with all the starry effects thanks to H.G. "PROOF" has told you about the A.I.R. and the dust from the moon in our bodies from the very breath we all share. Now you understand the "PROOF;" you cannot live without your hypothalamus gland.

The H.G. being different in the male and female; but let's go into detail in this phase of the dance between Wo and Mann. "PROOF" turned the names around because the two together competes them as a pair "WO-MAN! The H.G. of Wo during the dance between her and Mann did more than make her feel good; dopamine was making things slip and slide for the acceptance of more than their skin.

Travelling through both of their nervous systems; dopamine controlled the movements of the cellular activities taking them from point to point of no return. Even a rocket scientist understands that Mann has the form to fit inside of Wo; and Wo has the form to fit around Mann's, however we say "man and Woman" when we refer to them in our speaking. In this book, Wo is only half of Man; together they are complete. Wo is complete with her other half with Mann. H.G. takes what is only their half in each other and cajoles them together in ways that only God involuntarily will do.

H.G. takes Wo and Mann's very molecular cells within them and energizes them to a life change result. A result that only begins in two different H.G.'s, but through the magnetic energy of the H.G., Wo and Mann attract and dance the dance of life, and then the involuntary action of the H.G. cajoles the deoxyribonucleic acid within Wo! Let's take a peep inside Wo's body right after the dance between her and Mann.

The pituitary gland has been given the signal from the H.G. following ovulation, to release an ovum this month, from Wo's right side fallopian tube; cell to cell communication is critical for survival of an organism as in this process, the fimbriated, or finger-like, end of the Fallopian tube sweeps over the ovary.

It has reached maturity and is traveling towards the exit. Cells can communicate through a process called signal transduction pathway. When sending a signal, different molecules, such as hormones, can bind to a receptor on or inside the cell membrane, leading to chemical reactions in the cell ultimately reaching the target. Cells are a second messenger to transmit these messages. The dopamine receptors affect many various functions, ranging from hypertension and hormonal regulation to voluntary movements and reward. As soon as the egg is released from the ovary, it has about 12-24 hours to live.

If this life cell is not fertilized by a sperm during this time, it dies and is eventually shed with the uterine lining. Once again "PROOF" proves buried deeply within the brain located directly above the brainstem, about the size of an almond, not visible without dissecting the brain is the hypothalamus.

The hypothalamus secreting cellular energy hormone of **dopamine**; the "**life energy**" needed for the very movement of specific receptors, primary cilia which having adhesive sites on them, on the surface of the fimbriae responsible for egg pickup and movement into the tube! Life still holds its mysteries, yet "PROOF" be told; dopamine is the energy of the activities of every living cell to live and have and promote its activity.

The central and most important part of an object, movement, or group, forming the basis for its activity and growth is the nucleus; the positive central core of an atom. This nucleus containing nearly all its mass in a dense organelle present in most eukaryotic cells in typically a single rounded structure bounded, enclosed by a double protective membrane.

"PROOF" elaboration of the genetic treasure nested inside the nucleus of every eukaryotic cell describing several feet of genetic material, compacted chromatin spun like beads around a spool, roughly two times around eight small proteins called histone.

This entire D.N.A.-histone complex is called a nucleosome; a string of compacted necleosomes is called chromatin! Each of us has enough D.N.A. to go from here to the Sun and back more than 300 times, or around Earth's equator 2.5 million times!

Not all cells have a nucleus; those with a defined "true" nucleus (eukaryotic) and (those with no defined nucleus (prokaryotic). If you don't have a defined nucleus, your D.N.A. nucleoid having an irregular shape is not protected by a membrane and is probably floating around the cell in a region called nucleoid! Bacteria are prokaryotic!

The central part of an atom that is made up of protons and neutrons which being the most important part of something. The atom can be broken down into 3 parts; protons, neutron, and electrons. Each of these parts has an associated charge, with protons carrying a positive charge, electrons having a negative charge, and neutrons possessing no net charge.

The hypothalamus is a collection of nuclei with a variety of functions. Many of the important roles of the hypothalamus involve what are known as the two H's: Homeostasis and Hormones.

Homeostasis is the maintenance of equilibrium in a system like the human body. Optimal biological function is facilitated by keeping things like body temperature, blood pressure, and caloric intake expenditure at an average constant level.

The hypothalamus receives a steady stream of information about these types of factors. When it recognizes an unanticipated imbalance, it enacts a mechanism to rectify that disparity. The hypothalamus generally restores homeostasis through two mechanisms.

First, it has connections to the autonomic nervous system, through which it can send signals to influence things like heart rate, digestion, and perspiration. For example, if the hypothalamus senses that body temperature is too high, it may send a message to sweat glands to cause perspiration, which acts to cool the body down.

The second way the hypothalamus can restore homeostasis, and another way the hypothalamus can influence behavior in general, is through the control of hormone release from the pituitary gland. The pituitary gland is a hormone secreting gland that sits just below the hypothalamus.

It consists of two lobes called the anterior and the posterior pituitary. The hypothalamus secrets substances into the bloodstream that are known as releasing hormones. They are so named because they travel to the anterior pituitary and cause it to release hormones that have been synthesized in the pituitary gland.

Hormones released by the anterior pituitary due to signals from the hypothalamus (and their general role in parentheses) include growth hormone (growth), follicle-stimulating hormone (sexual development and reproduction), luteinizing hormone (testosterone production and reproduction), adrenocorticotropic hormone (stress, fear response), thyroid stimulating hormone (metabolism), and prolactin (milk production).

The hypothalamus also synthesizes a couple hormones of its own: oxytocin and Vasopressin. These are then sent to the posterior pituitary for release into the bloodstream. Oxytocin can act as a hormone and a neurotransmitter.

It has important roles infacilitating childbirth (hence the use of Pitocin to induce labor) and lactation, but also has been the subject of a lot of recent research due to its hypothesized role in compassion and social bonding. Vasopressin's main functions are to control urine output and regulate blood pressure (although it also seems to play a part in social and sexual behavior).

The hypothalamus thus has widespread effects on the body and behavior, which stem from its role in maintaining homeostasis and its stimulation of hormones release. It is often said that the hypothalamus is responsible for the four F's: fighting, fleeing, feeding, and fornication. Clearly, due to the frequency and significance of these behaviors, the hypothalamus is extremeness important in everyday life and as in the physical bodies of Wo and Mann!

The clock is ticking, the race for the egg now being carried downstream by the cellular activity of the cilia empowered by the life-energy of dopamine; secreted from **Wo's "Motherboard"** we all know is her hypothalamus!

Since there is a difference between Wo's and Mann's H.G., it has continued to secrete the involuntary action in the stream of cellular life energy starting their puberty; and now after their dance of love has reached its peak. Wo's ovum having 23 chromosomes as in each sperm of Mann's; cajoled with the spirit of **life energy** positively charged to a mutual concept!

How sweet it is to be loved and getting along together on one accord! Once the dance is physically over and our bodies have untangled; life goes on, and indeed, it does for Wo and Mann.

Sperm production is hormonally driven. Brain hormones govern sperm production and are precisely controlled. Mann's genitalia are responsible for sperm and ejaculate production within the brain. The H.G. and anterior pituitary control sperm production.

Sperm is made from precursor cells termed germ cell that give rise to approximately 120 million sperm daily in a process termed spermatogenesis that takes approximately 64 days in humans. This is equivalent to making about 1,200 sperm per heartbeat. Despite the high-volume production of sperm, quality control checkpoints exit throughout the sperm production process to ensure the biological and genetic integrity of ejaculated sperm.

It has been long believed that sperm takes 90 days (3 months) to be made and ejaculated; "PROOF" will tell you updated understanding that sperm develop in the testicles for 50-60 days and then are excreted into the coiled ducts of the epididymis and complete their maturation for another 14 days. Sperm waiting to be ejaculated remain in the epididymis near the bottom in the scrotum.

At ejaculation, 500, million sperm are propelled through the vas deferens within the spermatic cord and into the abdominal cavity and join the seminal vesicles, which add alkaline fluid that helps to support sperm. The ejaculate consists of fluid from 3 sources.

The vas deferens (sperm fraction). the seminal vesicles, and the prostate. The seminal fluid makes up 80% and the prostate gland another 10%. This mixture of semen then exits the penis during ejaculation.

Wo and Mann have introduced themselves in skin to skin in their physical dance and now it's time for the Egg and the sperm to take the dance floor; but what is the egg and what is the sperm? "PROOF" will answer those questions with a bit of drama! Man was made first; so, let's be respectful and give rise to the sperm!

The spermatozoon is a remarkably complex metabolic, locomotive and genetic machine. It is approximately 60 microns in length and is divided into 3 sections. Head, neck and tail. The oval sperm head consists of a nucleus containing the highly compacted D.N.A., and an acrosome that contains the enzymes required for penetration of the eggshell for fertilization. The neck maintains the connection between the sperm head and tail and consists of the connecting piece and proximal centriole.

The tail harbors the midpiece. The tail midpiece contains the axoneme or engine of the sperm and the mitochondrial sheath, the source of energy for movement. Physiologically, the sperm axoneme is the true motor assembly and requires 200-300 proteins to function.

Among these, the microtubules are the best-understood components. Sperm microtubules are arranged in the classic "9+2" pattern of 9 outer doublet. Defects in the sperm axoneme are well recognized causes of ciliary dyskinesias that are routinely associated with infertility.

Much can and will be said about the sperm, but "PROOF" must share information as well about the female egg. Follicles are fluid-filled structures in which the oocyte (also called egg) grows to maturity. Every female fetus, including your mother, developed all the eggs (none are male sperms, females don't have male cells) she will ever have while a fetus still inside of her own mother. Not to any surprise to "PROOF" that one of those eggs ultimately developed into you!

So in reality, you were passed down as an egg inside of your mother from her mother (*your-grandmother*) and every mother in your family tree passed down the same eggs to their daughter to birth the daughter she didn't birth for as far back from that life energy that has dazzled all of our conceptions as daughters! Current knowledge indicates that females are born with their entire lifetime supply of gametes.

At birth there are approximately 1 million to 2 million eggs; by the time Wo reached puberty, only about 300,000 remain. Of these, only 500 will be ovulated during her reproductive lifetime. The fewer eggs a female has in her ovaries, the lower her odds for conception.

The egg cell or ovum is typically not capable of active movement, and it is much larger (visible to the naked eye) than the motile sperm cells. When an egg and sperm fuse, a diploid cell (the zygote) is formed, which rapidly grows into a new organism.

"PROOF" stands for truth even when truth is denied; as it has been for years, even as people turn their faces and refuse to admit that O.L.B.A.C. Nevertheless, life energy goes on as the sperm cells of Wo and Mann are given censored hormonal energy from each of their prospective hormones.

Early that very morning Wo felt the egg released from her ovary; In this month's cycle her right fallopian tube twanged with the electron's energy. Her central nervous system messaging her brain, as she registered twinges and cramping; but she hardly gave it more than a passing thought. Wo's egg has 24 hours of life energy to wait for the sperm and be fertilized.

"PROOF" knows that the ovary of the right-side yields ova which on fertilization develops as males, and the ovary on her left side yields ova which are potentially female! From now on, you will not have to guess whether it will be boy or a girl; just check the side you feel your egg release from! Of course, dopamine has the credit and honor due from **sparking the energy** and cellular motion for the release of that golden egg!

Wo is all smiles and dreamy eyed while curled up all cozy in their bed; she could hear the shower running as she turns over alone in their king-sized bed. Mann shaved and smiled the same "smillinginsideoutsmile" as Wo. Thoughts of how much in-loved they are together; even in silence!

"PROOF" is so excited about the inside dance going on inside of these lovebirds; there is so much happening! The last thing "PROOF" was telling you about was the egg waiting for her concept with the sperm.

At this particular timing deep within the fallopian tube, there wasn't a sight of just one of the *499 **million of expendable*** *suitors; never the less, the best was the one sperm that was meant to be the only one to concept with this one egg was on his way!*

Almost 50% of all marriages end in divorce in the U.S. "PROOF" will prove that even the ones that stay married; the percentage of them being "joined by "LOVE" is the same ratio as the sperm race, they came from, even worse.

There are about 2 or 3 more men in this world than women; but out of 157.0 million females, just one that would be the only female that would be chosen by the hypothalamus gland as a man's wife for life!

NOW, YOU CAN SEE how "PROOF" PROVES THAT EVEN THE 99.9% THAT STAY MARRIED ARE NOT happy because they are not "Spiritually joined together "Inlove." "PROOF" also proves why people cheat and will continue to have a wondering eye and heart with empty feelings without that one person.

Feelings as well as the promises made to be broken as your own words trap you on recycled paper given to whoever "takes" someone "IF" they were not "JOINED" by God. The law made by the people being just as blind spiritually as mice; "PROOF" proves they can't guarantee love, feelings of lasting devotion, they are missing something in "just" a law marriage; they really are, that one in a 157. Million that only God will give to a man!

You can fool some of the people for so long until you end up being fooled. You can't fool most people and never God. My coffee is sitting here, and I think I better take a break. One more thing, "PROOF" was asked to be written; and I am just telling it like it should have been told to you by someone who knows the truth. When you hear the truth, it will set you free or you run from the truth hiding and continue to fake happy being miserable, joining the crowd.

Conception *is* our beginning in life; "PROOF" will prove that is true, but there are more than one conception to our beginning, however, it is not like you have understood. This will be my "Authors' notes:

A "Spiritual" conception being the joining of the male and female (our parents) together "Inlove." Then there is the **"Physical" conception**, where the genitals come together in an intimate dance. (some couples start at this level)

The "Chemical" "Our" conception is when the female pronucleus and the male pronucleus come together inside the egg; O.L.B.A.C. "PROOF" is going to tell you the biased truth, which in this case has never quite been told in this fashion before; but it's the "PROOF" and the truth, so help me God to tell this truth with Medical, Scientific, Biblical and Godly "PROOF!"

PHASE 2

CELLULAR MOVEMENT!

"PROOF" HAS CALLED them by their birth-names "Wo & Mann;" but suddenly A.I.R. preserved this time to fuse their locking sweltering, melting skin. Their very pulse pounding and quickening in tuned with the activating nucleic activity of the cellular energy deep within their sugar phosphates and nitrogen driven by dopamine and the hypothalamus gland!

Positive *life-energy* coaxing with the negative energies; sparking their bodies with a magnate force, drawing them skin to skin! Beyond anything that they could every ask or think; stretching beyond one's scope of imagination lays 2 hearts beating together as one; a defined nucleus forming their own "WoMan" complex! Wo & Mann; ("WoMan") nested together spun like thread, spooled around each other in a physical dance of "Soulove!"

"WoMan," one true nucleus; eureka! Can't we all just get along? The K.J.V. says; there will be wars, and rumors of wars, but the end is not yet! "PROOF" proves that the war against the sperm and the egg has been going on and recorded as far back when a man chose to spill his seed upon the ground than to give it life within the egg!

Birth control has utterly intercepted and became the slayer of life energy interceding, misleading and disconnecting the circuits of bonding in every generation! The war is lost in the separation abilities in the forces of death against life; the space between sperm and the egg can result in the death of a family, a generation gap and even a loss of a nation!

The future of one sperm and one egg depends upon the positive and the negative coming together through the sheer life energy and the will to bond together in peace through not of shedding blood, but by 23 chromosome coming together of each between one sperm and one female to make one whole person of 46 genes!

Faith to persevere continues as the war within; a war where the lives of millions been counted as for the slaughter, and the remaining few that still stand are yet to die leaving just one to satisfy quest of life energy for the egg! The female "Motherboard" has already secreted thinned out mucus at the time of ovulation, aiding the sperms when they swim upstream once inside her walls of her vagina.

Her motherboard has already made preparation for this expected passing of 500, million sperms! Now is about the best time as ever to "PROOF" you about "Sperm!" Sperm, also called spermatozoon, plural spermatozoa, male reproductive cell produced by most animals. The sperm united with (fertilizes) an ovum (egg) of the female to produce a new offspring. Mature sperm have three distinguishing parts, a head, the midpiece, and a tail. The tip of the head of the sperm is the portion called the acrosome, which enables the sperm to penetrate the egg; Mind you "PROOF" did not say "crack" the egg.

This is not a laughing matter, but I had to put that *pun* in there! The sperm cells literally must fight their way through the three layers, first using chemicals contained in their acrosome, and then using a spike on their head to puncture a hole as the sperm forces its way forward by thrashing its tail. "PROOF" has one more detail to add to this dominate male sex tool; men have lost the D.N.A. code that once made human penises spiny.

This would add insult to injury! This is a dance mind you and all is fair in love and war, **without the spikes**, please and thank you! I just have to say that this would be a perfect case for breaking and entering, or even battery and God knows this is the truth; "PROOF" describes this headpiece that the army of 300+ million sperms are wearing; pure intimidation which is not going to go over very hospitable with the "Mother-broad" or "Motherboard."

From the very beginning of this dance between Wo and Mann; the love-dance between the sexes was meant to begin as well that ends in a love-dance as well!

Wo's egg has about 6 hours to live, the H.G. supplying loaded armed ammunition that being 500 million sperms about to be ejaculated out of the vas duct of Mann's penis cocked as a fun-loving persuader and invade into the surface of the vagina of Wo. Mann's penis is cocked as a fun-loving persuader.

The female "Motherboard" will not be defeated; dopamine comes to Wo's rescue to take action as "PROOF" will astound you! The vagina is invaded first by Mann's penis; the vagina is sweating silk love under the seducing powers of Mann and his sweet pillow talk, suddenly her vagina is attacked; 500 million missiles trespassing within a valley of death. There within the laced warm acid thick as mud flowed the quiet ebbs to sink, swim or die; 499, million counted as sheep for the slaughter against the one odd sperm that will live!

The war will be won; victory is peace, in our life that begins in "conception!" "PROOF" will be fair and continue to tell you about the midpiece of the sperm; this part is packed with mitochondria. Mitochondria are organelles in cells that produce energy.

Sperm use the energy in the midpiece to move. The tail of the sperm moves like a propeller, around and around. This tail is a long flagellum that pushes the sperm forward. A sperm can travel about 30 inches per hour. This may not seem very fast, but don't forget how small a sperm is. For its size, a sperm moves about as fast as you do when you walk briskly.

"PROOF" will have to explain things quickly, as life-energy from the H.G. alerts the cellular activity made during the dance between Wo and Mann.

A man may ejaculate 500, million sperm, which start swimming upstream toward the Fallopian tubes on their mission to fertilize an egg. Fast -swimming sperm can reach the egg in a half hour, while others may take days. The sperm can live up to 48- 72 hours. Only a few hundred will even come close to the egg because of the natural barriers that exist in a woman's body.

The female's motherboard has already made preparation to welcomes her guests with sugar phosphates mixed with a little bit of acid! It takes about 24 hours for a sperm cell to fertilize an egg. When the sperm penetrates the egg, the surface of the egg changes so that no other sperm can enter, now of conception, the baby's makeup is complete, including whether it's a boy or girl.

"PROOF" holds up her right hand of fellowship and female honor that the truth of the matter here has not really been told in the dramatic way that will be told by "PROOF!" "PROOF" is not sexist, or a libber, or anything of the like, but let the truth be known that the hypothalamus gland played a lot of favoritisms with the hormones here and there; a boost for nursing mothers, yeah for oxytocin an important hormone for women!

Men get females pregnant, men assist females while we labor in birth to give birth, they don't breast feed, but men do have orgasms, and so do females; men can have orgasms faster, but females have deeper and longer ones!

What "PROOF" has to say about the truth of being short changed is not in the oxytocin, but in the real fact that males are faster swimmers even as sperms; they usually are the first to arrive at the egg, within 1 half hour ready to do damage. "PROOF" Acknowledges the hormonal action producing millions and millions of sperms in the first place against just one little egg of the female that only could live 24 hours at the most, having no ability to move!

"PROOF" Acknowledges the soundness of reducing the troops down to 300,000 energized armed sperms. Every one of those 5 hundred million sperms are looking for trouble and; PROOF" will be more than happy to spell out the truth! If the sperms remained inside their own territory being that of the male's body, all would have been well; they all could have been singing war songs and 99 bottles of beer on the wall!

Where was **Noah** in all of this? A sperm named Noah was saved from the flood in the K.J.V., just as in this flood but only this is a flood of 499 hundred million other sperms ejaculated into a foreign body. Every healthy sperm doesn't always make it through the competition within the ejaculation; as some sperm just jump the whole process of being ejaculated.

17% of pre-cum contains a significant amount of healthy motile sperm that escape in this moment of pleasure even without ejaculation! This reminds me of Jonah in the K.J.V. trying to escape the will of God; yet he was saved as he was thrown overboard the boat and still, he was permitted to do what God had planned for him to do in the very first place.

Jonah hops a ride in the opposite direction, curl up take a nap. Then when he was corner in the ship being the cause of troubled waters; he rather attempt suicide then to face the fears of standing all alone against the enemy. When he was thrown overboard; a great fish swallowed him up, and God did things so well, Jonah never hit the water. The fish jumped up all excited like whales do; blew his stack and while he was up in midair swallowed Jonah all in one motion!

What an inter-ception! Game changer! conception! "PROOF" no body plays sports like Jonah and the whale. Actually "PROOF" proves that the whale uses a lot of energy to jump; it's not just for fun, or to put on a show, but to use as communication that carries a message! Obedience is better than sacrifice. You can run, but you can't hide. You can attempt to change your mind, but God doesn't change period. Jonah was not happy with God's will, but he got over it.

"PROOF" will tell you that yes, most definitely by chance sperm can wiggle their way through the fiber of those skimpy frilly layers of clothing laced with semen gliding their motility right into the slick mucus of the warmth of the vagina within 45 minutes of record timing and Erika!

Let the pregnancy test prove it to you with a reading that says "positive" this sperm was a "Noah!" I can imagine this sperm holding a S.O.S. sign when he fertilized the egg. Truly, this is not a time to be funny and telling jokes, or the likes; but only one sperm is needed to cajole and dance with the egg with or without being fully or half dressed, or taking off even before the gun was cocked, as you shall learn with "PROOF'S" understanding!

The hormones started sparking the physical seduction with flames of rewards as a dance full of kisses and caresses and all that heaven would allow between skin to skin with "WoMan!" "PROOF" can agree that Mann found pleasure as he would describe as "Heaven" inside the warm darkness of Wo that enticed them with surmounting pleasure all through this night long. Wo would just describe the experience as floating on the breath of their love!

The curvaceous female's body was made to receive the adoration and fit the asymmetrical rapacious splendor that of the male; but this is just the first part of submission on the behalf of the female. This giving in is involuntary; the female's response will be joyfully repeated once more as her body is persuaded and cajoled in passion and then invaded at the climax of this skin to skin dance during the ejaculation.

Inside Wo & Mann, an invitation of warmth given out by both bodies; estrogen lubricated Wo's vagina while her motherboard made sure the lubrication was warm while Mann's penis blended lubrication along with Wo's vagina from the testosterone hormone, all was done in pure bliss.

The penis of Mann is snug as a bug in a rug. Skin to skin, sunk inside the 6 inches of wo's warmth, and slickened velvet; as far as he can penetrate, then he feels the pleasure to explode, he holds this moment to take what is his pleasure. To give into this delicious feeling will open the flood gates of the urethra.

A hollow tube running through the penis that launch up to as many as 5 hundred million-minute men into the land where mortal man will never make footsteps, but morphs into another transformation; becoming invisible! Even though naked eyes cannot detect the invisible sperm; eventually, all but one trespasser will be killed, and acid from her own pleasure hormone will be spun as part of the trap!

"PROOF" is proud to exclaim that things are not always as unfair as they may seem; just wait and see how things turn out for the 3-500 million sperms as they leave their home and trespass into the uncharted territory of the female body! Mann was cajoled by dopamine along with Wo; dancing all night by mutual consent; but dopamine is cajoling more than what meets the eye.

Immediately after ejaculation, sperm can live inside the female body for around 5 days…during which makes the female happy; "PROOF" will tell you that women who were directly exposed to semen were less depressed; in other words, females are happy feeling semen inside them!

Once inside the female reproductive tract, where ultraviolet light is absorbed by the 500 million sperms re-emitting that energy as visible light, glowing their brightest on account of the particular mix of chemicals and semen which is composed of ingredients like vitamin C, zinc, protein compounds, cholesterol and sodium.

Heroic sperm in competition with each other; life-energy, dopamine controls the cellular activity! Sperm don't really swim straight, for the most part. Often sperm movement ability, known as motility, is classified into one of three groups.

Progressive motility; actively moving in a straight line or large circles. Non-progressive motility any other pattern except forward…. Immotile; not moving! Immediately the sperm cells must swim through the 3-7 inches of the vagina, reaching the cervix and into the uterus to reach the Fallopian tubes and female egg!

Here the "Motherboard of the female is silently spreading and working her magic potion as if the slow and the immobilized sperms were being hypnotized and all under the hormonal spell secreted from the control. This is a dance that one must not lose sight of ones' purpose; the battle is all uphill all the way, and as for as the sperms are concerned, miles to go without a moment to spare for rest!

It is a very long journey for sperm cells to make in just 5 days to live, and very few survive because the carpet (mucus) the female rolled out for the happy penis, is not so friendly towards sperms; in fact, the sperms are ejaculated in a very hostile environment where only the strong may go on, but for how long! During the dance, when sperm leave the penis, they don't head straight to the uterus

Sperm by the millions undetected by the human 5 senses suddenly entering the first and outermost portion of the vagina; on average 3-7 inches long. Progressive and some are non-progressive, and others are Immotile sperms cajoled again by the power drawing them into contact with cervical mucus.

The cervical mucus does two things: protects and rejects. It protects sperm from the vagina's acidity as well as rejects sperm whose shape and motility would otherwise keep them from reaching the egg.

Most sperm never make it to the egg for several reasons. To be considered fertile, not even 100% of sperm need to be moving, if 40%

are motile, and of that 405 not all make it to the egg. The shape has a lot of say in success. Having multiple heads, weirdly shaped tails, or missing parts can make a sperm simply unfit for the journey through the female reproductive tract.

While there are a limited number of eggs, sperm is available in a lifetime supply, but sperm production, or spermatogenesis, does take place indefinitely, but the quality and motility of sperm declines with age.

Older men are also more lightly to pass genetic mutations onto their children, about 4 times faster than a woman would. Underwear has (almost) no effect on your sperm, but boxers are a little bit more sperm friendlier, but it's up to whatever floats your sperm.

The cervix is the tissue between the vagina and uterus; the walls widen; a smooth fleshy O, about an inch in diameter. The hole in the middle of nowhere firm lips appearing to pucker up to the sperm entering its passageway, the neck to the womb of life!

Once the sperm have entered the uterus, contractions propel the sperm upward into the fallopian tubes. The first sperm, however, are likely not the fertilizing sperm. The crypts or cervix glands grow in numbers and increase in size to store more sperm. The cervix's mucus barrier thins out so it's easier for sperm to pass through. In this course, some attach to oviduct epithelial cells in the Fallopian tubes or get stored in tiny chambers called crypts until fertilization prime time; ovulation.

The Cervix a small, cylindrical canal that connects to the vagina to the uterus. Uterus or womb is where a fetus grows during pregnancy. Fallopian tubes are two tubes that connect the uterus to the ovaries, allowing sperm to move towards egg cells and fertilized eggs to move into the uterus.

Ovaries are two organs that produce egg cells that can be fertilized to become fetuses. Sperm can pass through the oviduct and end up in a woman's interstitial fluid surrounding the internal organs. What's so sad; sperm may literally float around in the body, never to be fertilized.

"PROOF" validates the war we each have struggled through from numbers far out reaching 300 million sperms dying silently as they *alone* struggled to maintain life energy within. Long before we felt the fire of A.I.R *scorch* our lungs; the very chemical that is very well known to medical and biologists to be the electrons in the hormones in the vagina, controlling the cellular energy moving along with the motility of the sperms!

We developed immunity to the hormonal acid that by nature of hostility morphed to being silent friendly fire; wave a flag of peace in the valley for just *one* warrior, neither brave nor strong.

Ask not what it is that your Mother will do for you after you're born but know what all she did before you were born. The very life energy caused a scab to form and you were just a scab. Each one of us as leaches burrowed into the lining of our mother's veins causing her to bleed. she bled for you. The wound healed, that became the second scab; then you were born. A scab from the wound as the navel healed; a permanent scar *chosen* by **life energy**!

Where is our honor from emerging into this atmosphere called earth? Our arrival was just another battle to live; forced to eupnoea, lest we die?

O.L.B.A.C. and the quest for life goes on from the valley of death in the pit-falls within the vagina, the cervix, and of our mother's womb to this vast sinkhole; we call home, in which we all continue to breathe air from which comes from A.I.R. flowing freely to each of us from the moon! "PROOF" proves to each of us that there is life here on Earth that appreciates the stars that shine and when they twinkle, they shed breathe for each one of us to live. Let us all thank God for the stars that shine and shed dust for our very own "gold breath mine."

PHASE 3

"MOTHERBOARD" CAJOLES SPERM WITH DOPAMINE!

𝕴T'S BEEN A long night; the night is still young for the sperms, but for the egg, the night is far spent, and the time of fertilization is still to be. Traveling the long road ahead has cost the lives of millions of sperms.

Only about 100 million sperms travel about 18cm from the cervix through the womb to the Fallopian tubes. 2.5cm about every 15 minutes, quite an army of brave, strong sperms.

Even though sperms may live for 5 days in the body of the female; the fastest swimmers may find the egg in as little as 45 minutes! Take it that sperm cells swim about 0.2 meters per hour, or about 8 inches.

These tiny objects that cannot be seen without a microscope being only 0.002 inch; but the egg is 30 times bigger, in fact large enough to be seen with the naked eye!

Thermotaxis and chemotaxis, Like the rays from the sun and gravity pull is to the earth; so is the egg's warmth and drawing to the sperm. The high temperature (called thermotaxis) areas of the woman's reproductive track where eggs are found, and higher concentrations of molecules released by the egg (known as chemotaxis) cajole the motility of millions of sperms by these 2 complex mechanisms.

Like plants in a garden growing upwards, drawn as in a trance towards the egg as if it were the spring sunshine. Millions of sperm motile in a behavior which in an organism directs its locomotion up or down a gradient of temperature.

The unmoving egg is in control by the female's "motherboard;" setting yet another trapping for the sperm that none of their armor can defend them against. The battle of life is a victory. The battle must be won not by togetherness in numbers, but by strength of the will of the involuntary action of **"life-energy."**

The life-energy of just one sperm-cell; energized by the male's hypothalamus gland's hormone called dopamine. The ever-ready life-energy shewing a warm light to the pathway to and by one egg standing alone and controlled by her hypothalamus gland's hormone called dopamine; "PROOF" Referring to the female's H.G. as "Motherboard-Witt!" How can the female lose with the seduction her "Motherboard uses?"

The warmth is drawing, the movement according to chemotaxis, a chemical stimulus cajoles the cell's movements right to the egg! The numbers of the sperm are getting smaller, but "PROOF" takes a closer look into the area and this is what is happening. Magnate attracts metal; there is more to be told about what's going on in the warmth and energy of the egg cajoling the sperm.

What has life-energy had to do with the attraction between the sperms and the egg going on here deep within the now 18cm pathway up from the cervix to the Fallopian tubes? "PROOF" proves that there is no doubt the head of the sperms are prepared for breaking and entering; but so far, millions of sperms have been lost.

Defeated, unchosen sperm; left dying without dropping their spear. The egg awaits within the tube; within her 11th hour, like the Sun at high noon, drawing the sperm inch by inch closer to the end of that equal to a 40-mile trip!

"PROOF" now proves that there is a conception for everything under the sun. Life-energy is nothing new under the sun; lust comes and goes around. What is started "Inlove" for Mann & Wo, stayed "Inlove."

God choose just one Wo for Man to be joined as **"WoMan"** by the spirit of love by the harmonious hypothalamus energy within us that is involuntary as the breathing and a heartbeat! In all the 300 million sperm; the involuntary action of both H.G.'s of the "Chosen" "WoMan," allowing one "Chosen" sperm to be cajoled in the final ***"dance with the egg to be joined -in-love-life-energy!"*** People dance as the world go around; but the hypothalamus and hormones choose who stays **"in-love"** after the dance, in the world as it goes around!

The hypothalamus gland secreted hormones of cellular activity from the very beginning of Mann and Wo; then they danced until that dance launched the 120 sperm out of the male's body as men into space, as perhaps the first true astronauts landing upon the "moon" of the egg!

Here the sperm prepared for battle unto death; yet be chosen to take the risks necessary in order to reach the egg; racing against all odds to blend a chosen deoxyribonucleic acid of the 23 male sperm's chromosomes with the life energy 23 chromosomes with that of the chosen egg of the Wo!

O.L.B.A.C. within the fallopian tube of our mothers; in this atmosphere we call earth. Our future generation will continue to breathe A.I.R. as life-energy is sparked in the tubes of mother's egg and father's sperm cajoled and suddenly O.L.B.A.C. for us all!

It is during the process of events **_that_** the oocyte initiates its final maturation of the division following the separation of the acrosome reaction of spermatozoa is a prerequisite for the association between a spermatozoon and an egg, which occurs through fusion of their plasma membranes.

After a spermatozoon encounters an egg, the acrosome, which is a prominence at the anterior tip of the spermatozoa, undergoes a series of well-defined structural changes.

A structure within the acrosome, called the acrosomal vesicle, bursts, and the plasma membrane surrounding the spermatozoon fuses at the acrosomal tip with the membrane surrounding the acrosomal vesicle to form an opening.

As the opening is formed, the acrosomal granule, which is enclosed within the acrosomal vesicle disappears. The dissolution of the granule releases a substance called a lysin, which breaks down the egg's vitelline coat, allowing passage of the spermatozoon to the egg.

The time of harvest has past, the egg has hardened her entrance; warmth of this solar system is not drawing the other sperm, the winter has come and the egg like the sun is moved farther from the earth.

The acrosomal membrane region opposite the opening adheres to the nuclear envelope of the spermatozoon and forms a shallow out-pocketing, which rapidly elongates into a thin tube, the acrosomal tubule that extends to the egg surface and fuses with the egg plasma membrane. The tubule thus formed establishes continuity between the egg and the spermatozoon and provides a way for the spermatozoa nucleus to reach the interior of the egg.

Other spermatozoa structures that may be carried within the egg include the midpiece and part of the tail: the spermatozoa plasma membrane and the acrosomal membrane, however, do not reach the interior of the egg. In fact, whole spermatozoa injected into unfertilized eggs cannot elicit the activation reaction, or merge with the egg nucleus.

The female pronucleus is the female egg cell once it has become a haploid cell, and the male pronucleus forms when the sperm enters the female egg. While the sperm develops inside of the male testes, the sperm does not become a pronucleus until it decondenses quickly inside the female egg. As the spermatozoa plasma breaks down; at the end of the process, the continuity of the egg plasma membrane is re-established.

The faith as in the size of a grain of a mustard seed! The spark of the hormone "dopamine" that as the faith of life in "love", in the beating heart, as in the first and continued breath; the hypothalamus is the faith secreting gland that does a body good and we just cannot live without as L.B.A.C., in all things pertaining to life, love and all living things! Life-energy is the faith that is gives us our life, love, cellular activity and our being! Just a little sugar and nitrogen is all we need, but without them, we would not matter!

Our life truly begins at conception; but understand what the concept of life is. The very con in life is in the energy that moves the very cells against all odds of gravity; as something within them that is more than we can explain, but certainty, there is life in every cell that creates the new being that continues separately in a new conception.

Life goes on; it just didn't just begin, life is energy that has an involuntary will of its own to create something new, make a new start with something unstoppable and undeniably alive. "PROOF" proves that life is a concept of energy; positive sweetness of energy when connects with the negative energy of nitrogen acid, a combustion where opposites attract, unites a bond called conception!

What is life? Again "PROOF" will use a nutshell of understanding; what came first the pulsing, beating heart, or the spark within the brain, or the life-energy of the hormone called dopamine? The very gland that we just can't live without; the hypothalamus gland that cajoled Mann & Wo joining by God's involuntary will in a spark of love. The hypothalamus gland administrates the body's homeostatic balances that is involuntary sparked by hormones.

God allows us to use common sense for our choosing; but there are also things that are never intended to be left up to our choice (Moses, led many astray with trying to do what only God's will never change in!) Marriage, intimacy in marriage, and children of that marriage.

God chooses Us, who he joins in marriage, and the blessings he gives in that marriage! This is a part of the involuntary action of God through our hypothalamus gland! You or I cannot change God's will, or His marriage, or the intimacy of the ones he joins, or the blessings He gives in those unions!

We have used our weak sensory such as our voluntary-walk-a-round-senses to pick life partners that fall down quicker than balancing the budgets during holidays when the most we make is less than 1% of a million dollars meaning even the budgets we thought was high income was actually not even on the level to be figured as 10% of a million dollars.

What would the millionaires do if they suddenly became "Thousandaires" (meaning they only had thousands of dollars in the bank instead of millions) then had to live off just 120 thousand dollars a year? Go figure! Most of the time, we can't even be assured to catch ourselves in a slip before we end up falling and receive fractures and what may have you.

God would not ever leave us to our own weak-minded poor judgement on such life issues as picking a life partner using our dim-witted 20/20 vision! Worst would God leave us to think when to breathe or to make our heartbeat! K.J.V. God forbid!

We must be given our breath, every breath by the involuntariness action of our hypothalamus gland under God's all-seeing eye! Every heartbeat, every major thing our body really need is balanced and supplied without giving it a single thought! With that life-energy of God's involuntary love blessing us His permission to be intimate! Life begins at conception, every conception that begins with "Love" or, "lust" is Life -energy!

Conception can begin without faith of "Love." If you have not been joined in love from God; then "love" has not made a conception within you and there is no **respect** of life that began in your conception! Nevertheless, "PROOF" O.L.B.A.C. began with the spark that was alive! Ever touch a piece of metal to a live wire? That's conception! The current is alive even if it has a negative result, by on purpose or by accident.

Lust has a weak negative result in the way we view the outcome of our lives; lust when it is conceived brings forth displeasure! Conception is the result of life energy. We all are called into a body; chosen to be who we are, winners, the over comer! We are stars of matter; alive, energized and occupying space breathing the A.I.R. from the dust of the moon.

While there are those among us who dream of going to the moon to live; where there is no light, no air, or heat; as others in waking moments wishing to breathe on life support machines just for dear life on earth, where air is plentiful and light is everywhere and the sun warms our atmosphere!

We voluntarily have free will to hold our breath when we make facial expressions of emotions and jesters in daily conversations and activities. With no thought of the hypothalamus gland keeping watch over the body's homeostasis. The respiratory rhythm directly and indirectly affects the central nervous system, which is affected during inhalation, thoracic pressure is reduced which affects the subarachnoid spaces.

We test our choice to challenge our involuntary reflex action by trying to control it, but our hypothalamus gland will not take bullying but for so long. There is a limit to even holding one's breath; the world's record is 11 minutes and 35 seconds!

"PROOF" proves to you that most of us have the ability to hold our breath for 30 seconds, but some of us maybe even 1-2 minutes; at this time our lungs giving the sensation they are being beat to a pelt by a prized boxer wearing boxing gloves fighting back delivering jabs that feel like your lungs will be burst with helium gas!

Something's got to give -in here; quickly this taunting becomes too painful to endure much longer as your nose flare and mouth gulps A.I.R. taking it in like an infant in his first breathe of life! Even if you were under water swimming in the sea, you're going to breathe! Breathing is a reflex action; we breathe more than 19,000 times a day automatically and without thinking.

We try to control everything! Just like children; controlled by our 5 senses; but God gave parents to be the involuntary action over the immature curious senses of the naive child. Changes happen beyond our control gradually; but puberty starts through the hypothalamus gland controlling the pituitary gland. That is out of our control. The hypothalamus gland works so hard at controlling such as the body temperature, emotions thirst, appetite, weight control, sleep cycles, sex drive, childbirth, blood pressure, heart rate, balancing bodily fluids and the production of digestive system all through life!

We find we don't want to control what we should; we struggle against the involuntary will within ourselves; going against that which keep us healthy and happy and balanced. We use chemicals for lack of self-control; but that does not make things turn out right from that which started out negatively out of control.

Using self-control is control. Self-control is birth control! Self-control is drug control. Your mind has a control to say no; but we use our common-walk-around-sense to cajole us into blocking out the control that protects us against perversions, volatile living, safeguarding our health and balance in our body.

That's when we have an unproductive desire to go against the grain; force a personal weakness over what we shouldn't engage in because we won't just say no.

There is a power of suggestion we all have with our finite minds; but the element of surprise is we are over-ruled by a power greater than our voluntary actions. we have our fate of our own individualized voluntary actions; we don't control God with our choices; God is not "controlled, persuaded, or out-witted!"

We don't control the hypothalamus gland that is working the perfect will of God's involuntary will without impairing and impacting the health and happiness in our bodies and life.

It's true, opposites attract; but without the involuntary will of the hypothalamus gland, we submit to the simple walk around sense that alter the health and happiness in our lives as well as the wellbeing of others as well.

O.L.B.A.C., but we still want to play God with our volunteer actions with our walk around common sense, trying to control the will of this involuntary action that has never been in our hands ever! "PROOF" asks you this question; "does life begin at your control, YES, or NO?" O.L.B.A.C., but not at your control.

"PROOF" proves we try to put our ducks, before the "QUARTS." This may be waaaaay over your head; but keep reading, just maybe your duck will fly back and get in line with what "PROOF" proves is fundamental before you start putting the cart before the horse!

A control that is not in our common-walk-around action; it is indeed in the control of the hypothalamus gland that works the involuntary action that is directed by God's hand in God's own timing, and in God's own way!

"PROOF" will admit that we do seem to take "matter" into our own hands, at least that's what we appear to be doing when we hijack, alter, manipulate, duplicate and even abort the quarks that are invisible and never seen with our eyes; these smallest particles that build and bond the protons with electrons together with zero neutrons!

Cain was conceived through Adam's disobedience (Gen. 2:16 Eve had not been made!) from using his walk-a-round-common-sense (eyes), (Gen. 2:18 what Adam did before Eve was made was not good) that caused Adam and Eve to be disgraced in the eyes of God; and again like the Sons of God using their eyes lusting after the Daughters of men and took them as wives setting themselves out as marriage in the eyes of the people. This angered God to the point of their destruction. Obedience is better than destruction, K.J.V.

Using one's voluntary actions for reproduction choices is totally against the holy will of God; a disobedience resulting in major consequences of personal mayhem along with mental, social, spiritual, financial sickness, disease and even death.

A many of us have paced and walked the floors, trying to deal with the stress of life-energy when we realize that "LOVE, MARRIAGE, and REPRODUCTION, are not-ever in our control! We lust, take partners and decide when to have a child; but God's ways are not like our ways and His thoughts are far above our thoughts.

"PROOF" proves to you that there are only three things that will anger God to our destruction; ungodly marriages, the ungodly sexual behavior, and reproducing of one's deoxyribonucleic acid without God's will! Love is the spirit of God; intimacy is the joy of God and children are the blessings from God to become strong together as taking the best of the two persons married and making them stronger in all the positive genes in a new conception!

CHAPTER ZERO HOUR

"PROOF" WILL BE the book to tell you that what you see is not what is always up front! "PROOF" has the back up from all points; Medically soundproof that you cannot see atoms with our naked eye. Biologically every living thing has atoms which are invisible to the naked eye. The Bible reads with a clause from a verse that "PROOF" adds with the facts that "you have eyes, but you see not!"

There is only one statement that poses a question to you as the reader; since we can't see atoms, and we can't see the particles inside the atoms that make up our cells of deoxyribonucleic acid, but they are there, do you still live life thinking you can control major life energy with your everyday walk around senses?

There are major consequences to disrespect the very powers by which life energy always plays rules; even to the point of being cruel and making your choices pick you as being the fool. Be still and know that God is God is one thing that even a child needs to be restrained by his parents he can't get for himself. But we mostly behave as children with our common walk-a-round-sense!

What are walk-a-round-common-senses anyway? That's an old saying that "PROOF" got from the older generation! Of course, it will be explained to you without you thinking twice. It is amazing these days the number of people who do not use common sense in the way it is to be used.

What is involuntary reaction is one thing, but what is common sense voluntary action is quite another. We need to have them both working together in our body; in our voluntary actions in our daily walk, or dance, hop, run, skip or sit around lifestyle that's a thing we all have common.

We as like the 500, millions sperms ejaculated into this place all in competition against each other; but only one is chosen! All together we try to outdo the other using strength and speed; but the race is not given to the strong, neither to the swift, but to him that is chosen from the very beginning by this involuntary orderly way without our choice in the matter. "PROOF" must prove to you that "Life has a will of its own and it's not what you think.

Thinking and doing is hard for some of us to do in our everyday life! It is easier to think we can walk on the moon than it is to do so; we must be qualified and that takes to be chosen. To be spiritually minded requires first to be chosen by God to "walk in the spirit." In the spirit there is no day or night; no light or darkness. There are no such things that have forms that appear. Everything is without form, invisible and all is seen through the understanding of God which is given through eyes of faith!

There are those, those such as of myself that have experienced "Death-Life experience." I know about things that is of peace and love beyond description; but unconditionally changed within for life! There is a knowing that goes far beyond telling; there is a light that natural eyes cannot vision. Love is an invisible positive proton energy that can only be released between the mutual negative electron energy and the bodies between them as a common ground.

There is a peace that rise from within, chemically bonding the two that once was, become as one and the half has yet to be told; life will never be the same! I must write my story about that one day; but, stay focused on the point that "PROOF" has to prove that some people, hopefully not you, but those other people have a tendency to not be able to walk without walking on your heels.

Those same heel walking people drive with that same foot that can't be controlled by common walk around sense, now is driving upon your bumper as they can't seem to slow down and judge the distance with their eyes by using their sense of motor skills of their voluntary action in their brain!

"PROOF" can prove what is life energy, where it is found, and where it is made; but remember it is invisible! "PROOF" must remind you in Chapter one; "WHAT IS LIFE?" "PROOF" proved that life is energy; energy that has an involuntary action of its own! You can't control this action of these <u>quarks</u> with your *"common-walk-a-round-quack-sense!"*

Immature people, young and the not so young as well as the swinging grand and even the great; are cajoled, seduced, and infatuated with music and drugs and peer pressure of sports and dare devil events such as the likes and the desire of "fitting in!" and even "Standing out!" What does "con" have to do with "PROOF" proving that O.L.B.A.C. "PROOF" began this book by asking a question; what is air?

This next question "PROOF" will ask is a leading question; not to mis-lead you, but to fully help you understand what this book of truth is proving about life! "PROOF" proves that our life began at conception but must ask you questions and then answer those questions! What does the simple word "concept" mean?

Let me sip on my coffee, while you ponder that with an answer. I must remind you that a lot can be understood about a word by sometimes dissecting it into smaller portions. "con" would be the first dissected smaller word; now let's learn what this word means!

To persuade to do something, typically by use of a deception. To con is to gain confidence or game by an instance of trickery or to hoodwink, bamboozle, inveigle. "PROOF" only used words to fully pull the wool that's over your eyes farther down; but you should understand when this word "con" means to "FOOL" or in the long run to "COAX!"

Even with our voluntary actions, we are coaxed; led to be persuaded to believe we are fully in charge and invincible; we hold our breathes and dive into the ocean, coaxed by our foolish walk-around senses, thinking that we will swim as fish! We have an involuntary reaction that is not playing our voluntary con games; you must take a breath, so hurry up to the surface for your life-energy lest you die involuntarily so!

Life plays a game all its own in the _"matter; positive and absolute zero, and negative_!" We all think we have a choice in everything about "LOVE, INTIMACY. AND CONCEPTION;" but, the game of life has its own rules, the bases are loaded; coax and take, and sabotage.

"PROOF" will prove what is sabotage. It isn't very nice. It's when you ruin or disrupt something by messing up a part of it on purpose. Your brain is your irreplaceable organ; you cannot live without it! You cannot live without your almond sized hypothalamus gland; but sadly, to say, by the time a child is reaching late puberty, the hypothalamus is damaged!

"Much known, much required; little known little required reads a passage from the King James Bible, but it appears that if you don't know anything, it appears you still will be required to be still and _know_ that God is God!

"PROOF" must hit this on the head of the nail so to say and remind you that the hypothalamus is controlling your pituitary gland to start puberty; so little boys can't make sperms before puberty and little girls can't ovulate before her reaching puberty, so it is now understood that this puberty is not a choice of our walk-a-round-common-sense!

"PROOF" must take another sip of coffee and prove that since little girls and boys were safeguarded by an involuntary action of the hypothalamus gland against conception; know that the very first Man to be given a mate was indeed in fact a Man; not a boy, so it was also a fact with every male in the Bible given a Wife as a Man, not a boy!

"PROOF" proves that medically speaking the brain takes years to fully mature; reaching ages of 40 years into adult hood! Adam was at least 100 years old when God gave him his Soulmate, and he lived to be 930! Noah was 500 years old when he conceived his first son, Abraham was 80 when he conceived his first child of promise. There is an involuntary action that waits for maturity.

Love comes with the striking sparks of maturity. Intimacy comes with the involuntary action of the hypothalamus gland; and conception comes with the involuntary action to the hypothalamus gland secreting dopamine under the strict orders of the divine will of God controlling "LIFE-ENERGY!"

It is the divine will in our involuntary action of our hypothalamus gland to cajole us by dopamine and not by _dope-a-mind, or "our common-mind!"_ "PROOF" proves that there is a way of thinking that seemeth right to us all in our own common-walk-around-senses. These ends are the pathway that is the _Broadway_, most traveled leading to, hell and destruction, and death!

Sickness, diseases, pain, tormented lives full of fear doubt and certainly unbelief; the happenings among the disobedient placed in slippery places of our choice, stuck in our common-walk-a-round-lifestyles. "PROOF" proves that God does not think; God knows! God knows what we think, and the pondering of our heart, as the meditations of thoughts before we think them; and yet we foolishly tempt God with our vain imaginations and then we cry unto God, and ask him to deliver us from out of all of our trespasses, and our evil mined ways, but Hell has enlarged itself!

THERE IS A TIME FOR EVERYTHING UNDER THE SUN

HERE IS A time for love and a time for hate (lust); a time to embrace and a time to refrain from embracing! Humans can only go as far as to bring future pain, disease, destruction lives in which destroy themselves, in relentless self-made tortures ending slowly and never admitting we are our worst enemy.

Life-Energy is the be all that creates all living things; the cause and the effect of living a new life. The solvent will of God has not changed; God change not! From the life of Cain that was conceived from using walk-a-round-common-sense (eyes), that caused Adam and Eve to be disgraced in the eyes of God; to the Sons of God using their eyes lusting after the Daughters of men and took them as wives setting themselves out as marriage in the eyes of the people.

This angered God to the point of their destruction. Using one's voluntary actions for reproduction choices is totally against the holy will of God without major consequences of personal mayhem along with mental, social, spiritual, financial sickness, disease and even death.

A many of us have paced and walked the floors, trying to deal with the stress of life-energy when we realize that "LOVE, MARRIAGE, and REPRODUCTION, are not-ever in our control! We lust, take partners and decide when to have a child; but God's ways are not like our ways and His thoughts are far above our thoughts. **There is a time for everything under the Heavens; K.J.V.**

THERE IS A TIME TO SCATTER STONES! At ejaculation, 500, million sperm are propelled through the vas deferens within the spermatic cord and into the abdominal cavity and join the seminal vesicles, which add alkaline fluid that helps to support sperm.

The ejaculate consists of fluid from 3 sources. The vas deferens (sperm fraction). the seminal vesicles, and the prostate. The seminal fluid makes up 80% and the prostate gland another 10%. This mixture of semen then exits the penis during ejaculation out of the approximately 1,000 sperm that enter the fallopian tube, only about 200 reach the egg.

The rest are attacked by the lining of the oviduct, or just give out; this is **_A TIME TO DIE!_** 499 million sperm lusted in vain after the egg; but only one, just one sperm was chosen, *and the "last sperm surrenders." In this battle, the strongest sperm of man is captured and taken prisoner of war until he joins forces with the ovum.*

THERE IS A TIME TO CAST STONES AWAY! Normally, only a single one-celled sperm cell can fertilize one egg cell, resulting in the development of an embryo. After the first sperm breaks through a layer of proteins around the egg, this layer blocks more sperm from getting through, but if too many sperm reach the egg, two or more, in rare cases sperm can break through this layer and end up fertilizing the egg.

This is called polyspermy. By delivering extra genetic material to the egg this increases the risk for D.N.A. mutations, brain conditions such as down syndrome, or potentially fatal defects in the heart, spine and skull. ***THERE IS THE TIME TO SEARCH!*** Propelled by the involuntary actions of the powers beyond its control to be one with the single egg! Each fallopian tube is 10-13cm (4-5 inches) long. The channel of the tube is lined with a layer of mucous membrane that has many folds and papilla, which are small cone-shaped projections of tissue. The cervical mucus acts as a reservoir for extended sperm survival!

THERE IS A TIME FOR PEACE! The future of one sperm and one egg depends upon the positive and the negative coming together through the sheer life energy and the will to bond together in peace through not of shedding blood, but by 23 chromosome coming together of each between one sperm and one female to make one whole person of 46 genes! It is during the process of these events that the oocyte initiates its final maturation of the division following the separation of the….

THERE IS A TIME TO DANCE! The acrosome reaction of spermatozoa is a prerequisite for the association between a spermatozoon and an egg, which occurs through fusion of their plasma membranes. After a spermatozoon meets an egg, the acrosome, which is a prominence at the anterior tip of the spermatozoa, undergoes a series of well-defined structural changes.

THERE IS A TIME TO EMBRACE! A structure within the acrosome, called the acrosomal vesicle, bursts, and the plasma membrane surrounding the spermatozoon fuses at the acrosomal tip with the membrane surrounding the acrosomal vesicle to form an opening. As the opening is formed, the acrosomal granule, which is enclosed within the acrosomal vesicle disappears. The dissolution of the granule releases a substance called a lysin, which breaks down the egg's vitelline coat, allowing passage of the spermatozoon to the egg.

THERE IS A TIME TO LOVE! The acrosomal membrane region opposite the opening adheres to the nuclear envelope of the spermatozoon and forms a shallow out-pocketing, which rapidly elongates into a thin tube, the acrosomal tubule that extends to the egg surface and fuses with the egg plasma membrane. The tubule thus formed establishes continuity between the egg and the spermatozoon and provides a way for the spermatozoa nucleus to reach the interior of the egg.

Other spermatozoa structures that may be carried within the egg include the midpiece and part of the tail: the spermatozoa plasma membrane and the acrosomal membrane, however, do not reach the interior of the egg. In fact, whole spermatozoa injected into unfertilized eggs cannot elicit the activation reaction, or merge with the egg nucleus. As the spermatozoa plasma breaks down; at the end of the process, the continuity of the egg plasma membrane is re-established.

THERE IS A TIME TO SEARCH! Propelled by the involuntary actions of the powers beyond its control to be one with the single egg!

THERE IS A TIME OF PEACE, TIME TO LAUGH, TIME TO KEEP! Only one 1 enters the egg to fertilize it. ***THERE IS A TIME TO BUILD UP!*** After the meeting of the egg and sperm, the fertilization occurs, and an embryo is created in the fallopian tube. After fertilization occurs, the ovum remains in the fallopian tube for about 72 hours.

Once an embryo is formed, it will undergo many divisions and go from a couple of cells over the next 5 days. By the time the embryo is a blastocyst (approximately 500 cells), it will be ready to implant into the endometrial cavity." (H.C.G.) ***THERE IS A TIME TO MEND!*** The ovum enters the uterine cavity for 60 to 72 more hours, and the central cavity begins to form.

THERE IS A TIME TO PLANT! A definite cell mass is formed on one side of the blastocyst by the time implantation occurs. ***THERE IS A TIME TO BE BORN; A TIME TO UPROOT, PLUCKUP***

THAT WHICH IS PLANTED, THAT IS OUR TIME TO BE BORN!!

"PROOF" proves there is a time to be born and a time to die, a time to plant and a time to uproot, a time to kill and a time to heal, a time to tear down and a time to build, a time to weep and a time to laugh, a time to mourn and a time to dance, a time to scatter stones and a time to gather them, a time to embrace and a time to refrain from embracing a time to search give up, a time to keep and a time to throw away, a time to tear and a time to mend, a time to be silent and a time to speak, a time to love and a time to hate, a time for war and a time for peace.

What do workers gain from their toil? I have seen the burden God has laid on humanity. He has made everything beautiful in its time. He has also set eternity in the human heart, yet no one can fathom what God has done from beginning to end.

I know that there is nothing better for people than to be happy and to do good while they live. That each of them may eat and to drink and find satisfaction in all their toil—this is the gift of God.

"PROOF" proves that everything God does will endure forever, nothing can be added to it and nothing taken from it. God does it so that people will respectfully honor him. Whatever is has already been, and what will be has been before: and God will call the past to account.

"PROOF" saw something else under the sun: In the place of judgement—wickedness was there, in the place of justice—wickedness was there. Tell yourself: God will bring into judgment both the righteous and the wicked, for there will be a time for every activity, a time to judge every deed: also as for humans, their carnal minds tests them so that they may see that they are like animals.

"PROOF" finds the wisdom of King Solomon stating surely the fate of human beings is like that of the animals: the same fate awaits them both: As one dies, so dies the other. All have the same breath; humans have no advantage over animals. Humans are the fault of Man; ignorance in the human heart is the curse of all human-kind; and the common-walk-a-round-sense- is the mockery of their folly!

Let them walk in their own ways, the gleam of their own understandings as the 499, million sperms all ejected into the lighted pathway of the gate that led to life; narrow is the way and broad is the road that leads to destruction, but only one, just one shall be chosen for life! In all thy getting, get understanding that we don't choose life, but life chooses us, before we were conceived; when we were all, but zero mass neutrons waiting for the involuntary will of God's zero hour when O.L.B.A.C!

Drugs sabotage the brain of a Nation's youth; if the hypothalamus is sick, the whole body is sick. I must sip my coffee; things are coming to a point of where no pun intended will make what "PROOF" proves as truth any easier to digest but is the missing link when proving that "O.L.B.A.C." is true.

"PROOF" will go back to the word "conception" and boldly state that life began with first a "COAXING!" "PROOF" proves that conception is part of a "COAXING" which is a "CON!" I am closing my eyes while taking another sip of my coffee; and now with wide eyed delight will tell you that conception is just a set-up, coaxing game!

"PROOF" must go on to proving what the other word means! What does "CEPT." mean? Cept is a Latin root word meaning "TAKEN." In this book "PROOF" proves that "CONCEPT" in the term "CONCEPTION" means "COAXED-TAKENED!"

"PROOF" understands that this is a little more than far-fetched, but, "PROOF" invites you as a reader to put any of these definitions together and watch your understanding shine with wisdom! Conception is truly a coaxing game; and "PROOF" asks yet another question, "who's favor is this game in?" The answer to this question would be a major part of this game. The deoxyribonucleic acid being the true contestants transported in the nucleus between the _"coaxed"_ sperm being "*taken*" by the egg, which has the upper hand, or being the thing that has the "favor!"

"PROOF" now proves that this whole "conception" is a lot more than what we've ever been told as part of what our life that began at conception is. Life that is energy; is just putting it simple when "PROOF" skips past the atoms; and avoid even the smallest particles inside the atom.

"PROOF" will not avoid what began at conception. The elements not mentioned in the process of life were truly invisible to the naked eye! "PROOF" proves that inside the atom, are 3 elements that are the smallest second to the quarks!

"PROOF" is saying "QUARKS" not quacks! No, I have not drunk too much coffee today; but I put too much honey in my coffee, but that's much to do about nothing concerning the fact that I still said "QUARKS!" Quarks, quarks, quarks, represent the smallest known subatomic particles. 2 up quarks, and 1 down quark These building blocks of matter are considered the new elementary particles, replacing protons, neutrons and electrons as the fundamental particles of the universe.

Quarks are made in stars! Quarks combine to form composite particles called hadrons, the most stable of which are protons and neutrons, the components of atomic nuclei. There are only 2 types of quarks that are necessary to build protons and neutrons; the constituents of atomic nuclei. These are the up quark, with a charge of $+\frac{2}{3}e$, **and the down quark, which has a charge of** $-\frac{1}{3}e$. **The proton consists of 2 up quarks and 1 down quark, which gives it a total charge of $+e$**

Quarks have their ducks all in a row and on a roll with a lucky strike! Quarks are electronic particles holding the deepest secrets of the universe of how all matter around us visible and invisible was created.

"PROOF" has proven what life energy is, where it is found, and where it is made; but remember it is invisible! "PROOF" must remind you in Chapter one; "WHAT IS LIFE?" "PROOF" proved that life is energy; energy that has an involuntary action of its own! You can't control this action of these <u>quarks</u> with your *"common-walk-a-round-quack-sense!"*

"PROOF" has not gotten carried away with the fundamental of the building blocks of life; but let's fly back and deal with quarts and our-common-walk-a-round sense! "PROOF" will prove to you, people only have this-common-walk-a-round-sense, even with high powered scopes or the such for x-ray vision; we still are near sited and farfetched from seeing the invisible spiritual world!

It has taken the medical, and biology field and scientists a world of forever learning and still not coming to the full knowledge of the astronomical consciousness hidden in the invisible elemental where the charges coax and cajole between themselves.

There are mysteries; things hidden and kept secret from since the worlds were formed, our eyes are dim and blind and cannot see with microscopes that are just as blind!

God is before all things; God is Alfa and Omega; The beginning and the Last. By God all things consist; whether they be thrones, or dominions, or principalities, or powers; all things are created by God and for God.

God is before all things visible or invisible. The invisible quarks are not hidden from the Spirit of God by whom all things are made naked and made manifested.

God is life; without God there is no living. God is the way; without God there is no going! God is the Alfa Atomic, Indivisible-Invisible-Absolute-Positive Spirit that MADE THE FIRST AND THE BEGINNING to be last; and the last and the end to be first; God be "PROOF" to be true and every Human a liar, and God be True!

(K.J.V.) The foolish things of this world yet confounds the educated, ever learning and never coming to the knowledge of the truth.

God made the quarks void of form, naked yet, willed within them the design mastermind to build the protons and electrons that bonded with the zero mater of neutrons that caused life-energy of conception, but "<u>LIFE</u>" (God) *did not begin at conception*; *<u>"OUR" life began at conception!</u>*

O.L.B.A.C.

EXPRESSIONS OF GRATITUDE AND APPRECIATIONS!

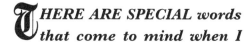 **HERE ARE SPECIAL** *words that come to mind when I think of whom I appreciate:*
EVERYTHING!
DESIRED!
Delightful!
Yes!

I thank God for being the Author and Finisher and the giver of all I am and more than I ever hoped to be; giving me everything desired and delightful and for the yes in my life!

To Sir Noah; my son, From the I.T. department. I adore and give you "Dopa Hugs" for building, customizing and maintaining my fantastic computer!

I express my sincere gratitude to My Marketing Executive Nick Mc Carthy, of my publisher for the inspiration of my book's Title; "PROOF." God revealed to him an "epiphany;" spoke to his heart and the life-energy of "PROOF" began at this conception. Your spectacular impression of the involuntary will of God; has begun to impact the world with its life changing realization. Nick, "PROOF" is a life changing "Aha!" book!

Vichyssoise of verbiage veers most verbose,
Author: Norah G, Wilson